LOVE AND FORMALDEHYDE

BY: C.M. GUIDROZ

● ● ● ● ● ● ● ● ● ● ● ●

Trigger Warning

Love and Formaldehyde is a Horror Romance novel. If you have ever been in love then you know it can get pretty horrific and doesn't come with a trigger warning. Lucky for you this story does, so if you are triggered by the following please do not read this book.

Love
Death of a Parent
Addiction
Sexual Abuse
Violence
Necrophilia
Murder

Explicit Content Warning:

Love and Formaldehyde is for ages 18+ readers. Some scenes are graphic, which means they get busy, do the nasty, bump and grind, get it on, get it in, and any other way of saying that the sexual scenes in this book are detailed and explicit.

Playlist

1. Cold Cold Cold- Cage The Elephant
2. Tear You Apart- She Wants Revenge
3. Please Please Please Let Me Get What I Want- Deftones
4. Who is She?- I Monster
5. Do You Want to Touch Me- Joan Jett and the Blackhearts
6. Lake of Fire- Nirvana
7. Love Buzz- Nirvana
8. Luna- Smashing Pumpkins
9. Romance- Varials

This book is dedicated to the people who still read for fun. Thank you!

Chapter One

Death.

We are all so scared of the inevitable end. I read once that dying is like a good book; you devour this book and enjoy it so much that when it ends, it leaves you wanting more. Comparing this to life would mean that your life was so enjoyable that you are left wanting more upon your death. I can not relate, which is why I have always been fascinated with death. My life has been anything but easy, and death seems like a well-deserved rest.

My eyelids grow heavy with the thought of rest and being out of this car. Finally, a small gas station breaks through the fog to my right, and I pull into the parking lot. Resting my head on the headrest as I park, I feel the tension release from my body. The building is barely visible in the thick fog surrounding my car. "Almost there," I say to myself; my own words fill the space. I have been in this car for over three hours, and as tired as I am, I'd drive another three hours just to put more distance in the rear-view mirror.

A burning sensation of guilt fills my chest as I remember who I left behind. I remind myself that I will return to take him away from that place, but first, I need to set us up. If I could have taken him with me, I would have, but there is no way I could offer him the stability he needs yet. I hated leaving him with her, but he knew I'd be back for him. My brother, Alex, is my motivation. When our dad died, it was hard on our whole family, especially our mom. We didn't just lose one parent that day; we lost both. She fell into a darkness so deep and hasn't gotten out since. I've always felt guilty for the time I got to spend with our parents as a fully functional family. I guess that's why I gravitated more to Alex, wanting to give him some sense of normalcy and security. The normality and security I felt before it all went to shit. That's why I got my degree in mortuary science and made sure to apply to jobs I knew were miles and miles away from home. After weeks of waiting, I finally got a job in a town hundreds of miles away.

The plan is to settle into this new town, make sure it's near perfect, and after a few months, I'll come back and pick him up. Then, Alex will come to live with me and never have to deal with her again. But first, I need coffee. The door to my car creaks as I open it. I can never be ashamed of my old beater car; she is my noble steed taking me away from the depth of hell. A bell chimes above my head as I walk into the small gas station. Making my way to the section with the coffee pots, I pull out a paper cup from the stack. My eyes stare into the black liquid as I fill my cup to the brim. I grab a red stirrer, even though I don't need it. I never add any sugar or creamer to my coffee.

"Good Morning, Gorgeous. You're a new face here. A pretty little new face." The man behind the counter doesn't try to hide his stare as I place the cup in front of him. The fact that he leans over the counter slightly to get a better view makes me roll my eyes. If I didn't need this coffee so much, I would throw it in his face, sit back and watch the steam as it burns his fucking eyelids off.

"Don't need to be shy now; I won't bite." He smirks.

"Oh, but I do," I say, leaning over the counter and giving him a view of my cleavage. "I bite, and sometimes when I'm feeling extra nice," I add a sultry tone to my voice as he practically drools like the fucking dog he is, "well, sometimes I..stab. Now ring up my fucking coffee so I can get out of this store. Is it you that smells like that, or did something die in here?" My tone turns harsh, and I almost laugh at how shocked he is by the abrupt change in my demeanor.

Leaning closer, I take an exaggerated whiff, "Oh no, that smell is you. You filthy little pig." My words have his face and neck flushed with embarrassment. Throwing a five-dollar bill on the counter, I grab my coffee and make my way to the front door. "Keep the change, buy a bar of soap, clean your filthy fucking ass. Then maybe try hitting on the next girl that walks in. I doubt it will work, but it's worth a shot. Have a nice day." I walk out the door, the bell chiming again as he watches me leave.

Moments ago, I wanted nothing more than to get out of the confinement of my car. Now as I get in the car and sit back, taking the first sip of coffee, I delight in the small space. I check the GPS and sigh at the relief of knowing I am fifteen minutes away from my final destination. Pulling out of the parking lot, I feel anxious, knowing I'm so close. Although, If this man is any sign of the type of men this town offers, I'll be happy to know that romance won't be a distraction at all. Luckily, I have several of my favorite men packed in the truck—fictional men, of course.

They don't make men like that in the real world. Men who don't mind a woman who can speak, think, or do pretty much anything on her own. I've met men who claim to love a woman that takes charge, but I've noticed that doesn't receive the same response outside of the bedroom. I have yet to meet a man that makes me feel anything other than disappointment; I know that sounds very "angry feminist" of me, but let's face it. I can only speak from experience, and my experiences have been less than appealing.

I want a love like Gomez and Morticia. Is that too much to ask for? Maybe even a little too cliche to ask for, given my "Gothic" appearance. But I want a true romance, someone who sees my darkness and wants to walk through it with me while holding my hand up to his lips. I will settle for nothing less, and that's why I'll remain loveless, single, and overall content. You can't break a heart that's guarded behind walls and walls of trauma.

The "Welcome to Ripville Falls" sign greets me, and I am hoping this is my new beginning. I know it's a lot of pressure, Ripville, but I need you to be perfect.

But I'll settle for safe.

Chapter Two

As I drive through the town, the fog clears, almost like it's unveiling itself just for me. Ripville Falls looks like one of those small towns you see in movies set in Salem, except it's in the middle of America. I've lived hours away and never knew this place even existed. The buildings are set up in a way that reminds me of a city, so close together with open doors welcoming you in. While across the street, there are beautiful Tudor- style homes with wrought iron fences and sidewalks. I look at the time, seeing it's nearly nine in the morning; the place looks like it's just waking up.

I hope I don't look suspicious as I drive so slowly, trying to take in the sights on both sides of the street. The homes and buildings are all in shades of burnt orange, mahogany, and various dark shades of black and bright gold. If my soul were a town, I feel like this would be it, and that fills my chest with hope. I almost forget to stop at the stop sign as I reach a four-way stop. Looking to my left, I see a building that catches my attention. The dark maroon bricks are being taken over by ivy growing up the sides. The tall building has two outdated-looking windows peering out from the top. A black sign with faded gold letters calls to me. "Bookstore" is all it says. The simplicity of its name fits the overall aesthetic. The owner didn't bother with a fancy, quirky name because this bookstore is not that.

Making a mental note to visit this place as soon as possible, I drive further down the road. An older woman props open her glass doors with buckets of flowers; her floral shop sits on the other corner from the bookstore. As I pass by, she looks up, and to my surprise, she waves. My mind forgets to wave back until I'm already out of her sight. I am not used to people waving and smiling, especially this early in the morning. The only thing you can expect from where I come from is stares, and if you stare back long enough, they will wave to you with one finger.

You had a set of unspoken rules in the town I left behind. Rules that you were never told; you just knew them. Don't walk alone at night, especially if you are a woman. Don't drive too slow unless you want someone to assume you're looking for something, usually drugs. The town was poor, underpaid, and forgotten. Drugs were easy to find if you were looking, everyone wanting to numb some variation of pain. We moved there once my dad died, and my mom couldn't afford to keep up the mortgage. Leaving that house felt like closing my dad's casket all over again, and I have hated her for it ever since. The fact that Alex was forced to go to a different school where he was bullied relentlessly only made me hate her more. But, now that he's fifteen, he's learned to take care of himself, keep his head down and stay out of trouble. Lessons I didn't have to bother learning in our hometown, where it was safe, and everything was still perfect.

"Your final destination is on the right," The GPS calls out to me, pulling me from my thoughts. My eyes take in the sight of the place I'll be calling home for a while. The small cottage, with its dark exterior and beige trim, invites me in as I pull into the driveway. I don't get out of my car right away; instead, I let my eyes look over every tiny detail. The big bay windows on both the bottom and top floor, the stone steps leading to the front door, and the sidewalk in front of the house surrounded by greenery all look so dark but still inviting. The landlord sent pictures of the house, but I had no idea just how amazing it was in person. Two stories, with two bedrooms, two bathrooms, and a small office that I plan on using for the library of books I have weighing down the trunk.

The familiar creak of the door seems louder in the quiet space of the front yard as I get out of the car. I'm not used to the quiet; I'm not used to peace. I had to fight so hard to get here, and while this may seem small to some people, it is beautiful to me. I'd like to think my dad would have been proud. Tears prick my eyes as I shrug them off and make my way to the front door. The landlord sent me the code to the lockbox in my email last night, along with lists of places to visit in town. She has become a friend in this past month while making this move much easier. Mrs. Janet is a fifty-year-old widowed woman who rents out her and her late husband's first home. What started as basic conversations on rent prices and location quickly turned into our favorite books and her fascination with my chosen profession.

I don't make friends easily; I am known for being standoffish and unfriendly, but as much as I tried, Mrs. Janet found a way through my tough exterior. Older people don't have the same anxieties or worries about asking personal questions; they tend to ask whatever they want. Most of the time, this can come off rude, in my opinion, but Mrs. Janet has a way of making it feel entirely different. Maybe it is the motherly way she asks or seems to care. Perhaps it's just my subconscious way of craving any type of maternal attention.

The lockbox opens to a set of keys that feel heavy in my hand despite them being so small. Unlocking the door and walking into the house, I'm greeted with the smell of old wood. I stop, inhaling the unfamiliar aromas, making me close my eyes and live in the moment for a while. This is the first time I walk into my own place. This moment of walking in and out of that door will become routine eventually, but not today. Today is the day I finally feel hope. Najeeb Mahfouz, an Egyptian writer, can be quoted as saying that home is not where you are born; home is where all your attempts to escape cease. Yes, this is only a rental, but to Alex and me, this is where the escape ends. This is where we can feel safe and happy again.

I allow a small smile to cross my face after what seems like months. Pocketing the keys, I take myself on a self-guided tour. The living room is big, with built-in bookshelves surrounding a dark fireplace. Mrs. Janet rents out the home fully furnished, which was one of the reasons I jumped at the opportunity to rent this place. The sofa and two armchairs are dark with an outdated charm. One bedroom sits off the left side of the house, while the other is upstairs. I wish Alex could be here so we could argue over which room would be ours. The office is right across from the downstairs bedroom, so I'll be making that one mine. The office is a small, cozy room surrounded by bookshelves. Mrs. Janet is also a lover of literature and said she and her husband spent many nights here, enjoying each other in silence. My heart feels a slight tug when I see the two chairs and ottomans set up by the window in the corner of the room. I can picture them reading next to each other, both escaping to different worlds yet still in the presence of each other.

After walking through the house, I stop to sit in the living room, throwing myself into the oversized cushions of the sofa. The drive and all these damn emotions have taken a toll on me, and I'm feeling the exhaustion pull me under. The loud ring of my phone makes me jump before removing it from my pocket. Before I can say hello, Mrs. Janet is already speaking.

"Dani, love, did you make it in town yet?" she asks, and I smile at her concern.

"Yes, I did. I'm just getting to the house about fifteen minutes ago. The house is even more lovely than the pictures you sent. Thank you." I reply.

"Oh, that's good, that's good. I'm sorry I can't be there to personally show you around today. But I'll try to stop by later in the week if that's ok with you. Are you going to need any help moving your things in? I can call around and get you some help." She offers.

"Oh, no. That's quite alright. I can handle it. I hope to finish most of it today, so I can check out that bookstore in town tomorrow." I answer, not wanting to socialize any more than I have to today.

"Now, don't be stubborn and hurt yourself. If you need any help, call me, and I can round up some help, ok? The only time I act like a damsel in distress is when there is some heavy lifting to be done." She laughs.

"Shame on you." I laugh, "But it's fine. I don't have much, just a few boxes. I'll be alright." I assure her.

She hangs up with me, leaving me with a warm feeling I'm not used to. So, that's what it feels like to have someone care. I know I won't be getting a call from my own mother to make sure I made it safe. I don't let myself think about it much; the anger I feel for her overshadows any self-pity I can come up with.

Chapter Three

The cool air greets me as I open the front door to start unpacking before Mrs. Janet decides to send some help over anyway. I don't have much to bring in, the heaviest being the many boxes of books. The first box isn't too bad as I carry it through the door to the bedroom. As time passes with box after box, my arms grow tired, so I start to unpack the few boxes I have already brought into the house. After about an hour, the house is beginning to look like my own. As I make my way to the trunk, one more box sits, waiting to be brought in. Picking it up, it weighs down my already exhausted arms. Suddenly, I feel the weight decrease quickly as the bottom of the box falls out, scattering the journals and books in the middle of the driveway. The relief my arms feel doesn't help the fact that now I have to pick all this up.

"Mind if I help?" a voice that sounds like gravel surprises me as I turn around to see an older man in my driveway. Dark eyes compliment the salt and pepper hair that seems messy yet sleek in that purposeful sort of way. While this man is obviously older, he has an instant effect on me. A classic, dark, mysterious air about him leaves me speechless for a moment.

"Sorry if I startled you. I was walking and kind of saw what happened." His voice finally brings me back to the current situation. I have a very attractive unknown man in my driveway, and I am standing here like an absolute moron. The way I eyed him down made me feel slightly bad for being so hard on the guy at the gas station.

"No, it's fine. I'm sorry it's been a long morning." I try to explain my complete absence of all human functioning. Before I can object, he bends down to pick up some of my things.

"It's fine; I can get it. I don't want to keep you from whatever you were doing." I don't recognize my voice for a moment. Fuck Dani, did you forget how to speak? I'm standing above him as I watch him slowly trail his eyes up my legs to meet my face.

"I assure you, my plans can be prolonged by just a few minutes to give you a hand. Is that ok with you?" he asks. I try not to smile at the way his words sound so smooth.

"Well, thank you. I appreciate it. It's the last box, of course, that would give me trouble." I say as I turn to close the trunk. "I can run in and get another box that one is broken." I let him know, but as I turn around, he has my things packed back into the box and is waiting for me to lead the way.

"I think I got it. I'll hold it from the bottom." He lets me know as he follows me to the front door. I can feel his eyes on me as I lead him into the house.

"You can set it down here." I gesture to the living room, not trusting him to go any deeper into the house. He places the box down and turns to me. The man dresses like he was plucked right out of an episode of Peaky Blinders.

"So, moving day, huh? Welcome to town. Name's Jasper." He holds out his hand to introduce himself. When I shake his hand, he grips mine gently; his hand feels soft as he releases mine.

"Dani," I tell him my name even though he didn't ask. "Thanks, by the way. You didn't have to do that." I let him know.

"Oh, nonsense. I couldn't let Edgar, Fitzgerald, and Morganstern just sit in the driveway like that. Besides, what kind of gentleman would I be to keep walking by." He says with a dangerous smirk. The fact that he took notice of what books he packed in the box makes me feel oddly naked.

"Great taste in literature, by the way. I'm an Edgar fan myself." He doesn't look around the house; he just stares right at me. So I decide to play with him.

"How do you know they are my books? They could be my boyfriends." I say with an equally dangerous smirk. This makes him smile wider, and now I feel like we are flirting. I don't usually say more than two words to strangers, especially men, and usually those two words are fuck off. Except for the gas station, asshole. So, the fact that this man has me being civil with him lets me know he has an effect on me.

"And so being young and dipped in folly," he dares me to finish the quote looking briefly at the ground before meeting my eyes again.

"I fell in love with melancholy." I finish the quote. I wish I could say I resisted, but that would be a lie.

"I thought so." He says with a smile. Then, after a brief silence, he speaks again, "Well, I should get going. It was very nice to meet you, Dani." He says before making his way to the door.

"Nice to meet you, Jasper. Thanks again." I say as I close the door behind him and brace myself against the back of it. What in the fuck was that? A dangerous distraction, that's what that was. I scold myself. I finally allow myself to feel the flush of my cheeks. What a pathetic woman you are, Dani," I say aloud to myself, rolling my eyes at how quickly I swooned over a damn stranger. An intelligent, mysterious, incredibly sexy, Edgar Allen Poe-quoting stranger, I laugh.

Suddenly a knock comes at the door, and my nerves are back on high alert. When I open the door, I see him standing in front of me again. Except now he looks a bit nervous.

"Sorry, I was actually going to grab a bite to eat. I know moving days can be crazy. I can, um.." He stumbles over his words and laughs nervously, shaking his head at himself. "Um, You are welcome to join me if you'd like. No pressure or anything." He says. The heat I feel pooling at the bottom of my stomach is screaming, yes, yes, yes. My brain interrupts, telling me I really shouldn't be getting involved with this man. It's my first day in town, and the last thing I need is to be joining random strangers for lunch dates.

"That's really nice of you. But I'm fine. I still have a lot to do here. So I'll just grab something a little later. I appreciate the offer, though. Thank you." I let him down gently. He doesn't seem bothered as he smiles and tilts his head at me.

"You're welcome, Dani, again. Welcome to Ripville Falls," He says before turning to walk down the driveway.

That could have been the smartest or dumbest thing I've ever done. As I close the door and make my way into the office, my stomach growls in protest. "Yeah yeah, I know," I tell my angry stomach. I'm starved, but I don't even know this man. He seems great, but he is not the distraction I need right now. I start to fill the shelves with my things. The more I unpack, the more the place feels like home.

After unpacking the few boxes, I had left, I can finally sit down to relax. Passing the entryway, the woodsy smell of Jasper's cologne still lingers a little, even though it's been almost an hour since he left. He really was a nice man. I'll have to ask Mrs. Janet about him; I'm sure she will fill me in on all the gossip. She has lived in this town for decades. He's probably married or an undercover serial killer.

The knock on the door startles me out of my thoughts. Standing up, I look at the door, realizing I want it to be Jasper knocking again. "What is wrong with you, Dani?" I shake my head. Get it together.

I look out the window on the side of the door, but I don't see anyone. Unlocking the door, I open it to find no one standing there. The only thing I see is a pizza box with a note at my feet. When I look up, I see Jasper just making it to the sidewalk as he waves his hand while still walking away, never looking back.

Smiling, I take the pizza inside and lock the door again. Anxious to read whatever note is on top, I place the pizza on the kitchen counter and fold open the piece of paper.

Dani,

I hope I am correct in assuming that everyone enjoys a slice of pizza. While you definitely don't seem like everyone, I do hope you accept these few slices as a welcome gift.
Also, if accepting food from a strange man worries you, I apologize. I didn't realize how bold a move this was until just now. I will not be offended if you toss it out.

Jasper

I laugh to myself at how painfully adorable this note is. I have to agree this is a bold move, and tossing it out would be wise. But I'm starving, and some risks are worth taking when you're as lazy and hungry as I am now.

This pizza is probably safe to eat, but there is no doubt that that man is dangerous. However, he managed to impress me, and that is not something that happens often.

Chapter Four

I thought the first night in the new place would make me nervous; instead, I was able to have one of the best nights of sleep I'd had in months. The light filters into the bedroom from the window, and I take a moment to enjoy the odd sound of silence. I don't hear the commotion from loud neighbors or horns blasting as I did at home. Home, that place was never our home. This is what home should feel like, peace and calm.

Checking the time on my phone, I see it is still early. I could go back to sleep or grab a book and settle into the office chair. The thought reminds me of the bookstore I saw in town. Well, now I'm convinced about how I will be spending this day. Today is the last day off before I start my new job, which reminds me I need to email the new boss that I made it here and I'll be ready to start tomorrow. Before I forget, I settle into the blankets and type out the email on my phone. Tomorrow will be my first day at this new job. I'm excited and nervous all at the same time. I've spent so much time, money, and energy on making a career path for myself. Finally, I can put my degree to use and hopefully make a life here.

Finishing off the email, I get out of bed and start getting ready. I have a plan for the day already in my head. First, I want to check out the local coffee shop, and then I'll head over to that bookstore. What better way to spend my last day off than to buy more books to add to my long list of books I still haven't finished yet. My phone chimes with a text message from Alex; I messaged him late last night to let him know I'm settled in.

Alex: Off to school. I found the envelope and hid it in my room. No, I won't spend it all on pizza and games. I promise. Maybe just one game....Kidding. I miss you already, loser. Love you.

I smile at his words, but my eyes fill to the brim with tears. I left him an envelope with enough money to help him get by while I'm gone. I have no doubt in my mind that he will be smart with the money. The fact that I could trust him with the money more than our own mother makes my stomach turn with anger. She would spend it all on booze or lend it to whatever scumbag she's seeing this week. I hate leaving Alex there alone; I fucking hate it. The day school ends, I'll be there waiting for him with the car packed and ready to go. "Just hang in there for a little while longer," I say out loud to the empty house. After texting him back, I grab my jacket and head out the door.

I could have driven to the shop, it would have been quicker, but I decided to walk instead. I need the fresh air to clear my mind. I have to fight the urge not to feel guilty for being here. I can't help but look around and feel so happy, only to have that feeling extinguished by guilt. How can I be comfortable and safe here while Alex is there? I know I shouldn't feel this way, but I can't help it. I repeat the same phrases I tell myself each time; You are doing this to create a better life for both of you. You are allowed to feel happy about this.

My mind is so far away that I almost pass the coffee shop. The building is on the corner, just a few blocks from my house. Mrs. Janet pointed out that this house is all about location, location, location. My house is just a few blocks away from the main street that runs through town. This street has all the restaurants and shops you could possibly need. Looking at the coffee shop, I think everyone in town came together and decided on a color palette they all must stick to. Like the rest of the buildings, the coffee shop is painted in a burnt orange color with exposed brick and big windows. The town manages to look old but modern at the same time, and I love it.

Walking through the door, I am instantly hit with the sweet smell of java. I can't help but take a moment to inhale the aroma before taking my spot in line. After getting my cup of coffee, I step back out into the cool air. The shops may all look similar, but they are very different in their own little ways. I pass a few antique shops before the sweet floral smell hits me. The flower shop I saw coming into town is open, with buckets of flowers lining the entrance.

"Good Morning, dear." A woman says as she puts a bright floral bouquet in the window as I walk in. I recognize her as the woman who waved at me yesterday morning.

"So, exploring the town today? How do you like it so far?" she asks in a pleasant voice.

"I'm sorry?" Her question catches me off guard.

"You're new to town, am I right?" She asks as she continues to fill the shop windows with arrangements.

"Sure, but is it that obvious I'm an outsider?" I say with a small laugh.

"Well, you have an antique beauty about you, if you don't mind me saying. A woman that looks like you is a woman that you remember. Seeing how I've lived here my whole life and I don't remember you. So you must be new." She smiles and takes her place behind the counter.

"I am, so you must know my landlord. Mrs. Janet?" I ask. She smiles big at the mention of Mrs. Janet.

"Oh, yes, I know, Janet. Everyone knows everyone here. At least all of us old birds do. We don't get too many new people here, though. You don't seem like trouble, so let me say,

Welcome. People around here call me Lenny, so you can do the same. I hope you are enjoying our little town so far." She says, and something about her voice is calming. She does remind me of Mrs. Janet.

"Everyone seems nice so far," I reply while browsing the arrangements. My mind flashes to Jasper, the silver fox that threw my defenses off yesterday. I'm tempted to ask about him, but I know it would be weird. So instead, my eyes linger on a small potted plant. The dark burgundy leaves are in a near-perfect geometric pattern. Beautiful.

"The black rose, or Aeonium. It's a succulent, so it would do well indoors. They will keep that dark color as long as they get a few rays in the summer." Her voice startled me; I hadn't even noticed she had left from behind the counter.

"I've never seen one like it before; it's beautiful," I say. I've never been one of those women with a dozen potted plants that they talk to and water daily. I barely had time to keep myself alive and thriving, much less a plant. Although, this one has me mesmerized. Maybe now I do have time for such simple luxuries.

"Well, it's yours. Please go on, take it. Consider it a housewarming gift." Mrs. Lenny offers with a smile.

"Oh, no. That's ok; I can pay you for it. I'm going to the bookstore, but after, I can stop by and grab it." I'm shocked yet again by the generosity of the people in this town.

"Nonsense, this is a gift. People don't pick plants; the plants pick them. I have never seen a more fitting pair than the two of you. Go enjoy the rest of your day, and I'll have it dropped off to you this afternoon." She says with a smile.

"That's very sweet of you. Thank you." I hope my words don't sound as awkward as I feel. I nervously take another sip of coffee before making my way to the entrance. I look over my shoulder, and Lenny is already working on something else and gives me a quick wave goodbye. She makes being happy, and content look so easy.

Stepping back out into the crisp air, I see my final destination for the day. I don't know if I can handle all this generosity and all these friendly people much longer. I have grown so comfortable in my defensiveness that having these people break that feels odd.

The bookstore is just as alluring as I remember from yesterday. I feel like I can already smell the books from where I stand outside. I take one last sip of my coffee before disposing of it and walking into the bookstore. Immediately, I am hit with an overwhelming feeling. Books are stacked on overflowing shelves all the way to the ceiling, towers of books on the floor, and dim golden lighting that makes you feel like you're in a book cave from some fairy tale. Yet, despite the overwhelming amount of books everywhere, the place feels cozy and warm.

"Welcome; looking for anything in particular?" a short man calls from behind the counter. I let him know I'm just browsing as I make my way around the first series of shelves. I'm instantly greeted with old paperbacks with cracked spines and a smell no one can replicate. Yes, I am a certified book sniffer, and this is my version of heaven. As I am browsing, I hear a familiar voice.

"Good Morning Mitchell, How's it going?" The familiar voice says as I slowly make my way around the shelf to see if the owner of this voice is who I think it is.

"Good Morning, Jasper. Slow start, but it's still early. I have that order for you. Let me go in the back and grab it." The short man I now know is named Mitchell leaves the counter to go into a back room. I watch quietly as the man who was in my entryway yesterday stands at the counter. The man dresses like he's from another time, so clean and dark. I try not to make a sound as I watch him stand there waiting. I wonder what he ordered, I'm tempted to go and say hello, but I know I shouldn't.

Mitchell finally comes out with a stack of books in his hands. "I also got another shipment the other day of.." He doesn't finish because as I strain to see the titles on the books, my foot trips over a stack on the floor, and I'm sent out of my hiding spot to catch my balance. I try to play it off, but I know I've been caught. I turn my back and look at the stack of books in front of me, but I'm not seeing a single one because I am silently cursing myself for being so damn clumsy.

"I'm actually in a hurry today Mitch, but I'll be by to check it out later in the week," Jasper says. I can feel his eyes looking at me, but I focus my attention on the books in front of me, hoping he just leaves. A few moments go by, but I don't dare glance over my shoulder just yet. Then out of the corner of my eye, I see him coming down the row towards me; I hurry and take a sidelong glance at him to find he isn't coming up to me at all. Instead, he is actually looking on the shelf for something. He must have seen me stumble earlier; I wasn't exactly quiet. But, on the other hand, maybe he doesn't recognize me from the other day.

My ears feel hot, and I'm trying so hard to concentrate on the book in my hands. Why does this man make me so nervous? I mean, sure, he's the most gorgeous man I've ever seen, but he has to be in his forties. Would that much of an age gap bother me? Asking myself this only makes my nerves even worse because, of course, it wouldn't bother me. I tuck my hair behind my ear and sneak another glance when he appears to have found what he's looking for and grabs the book from the shelf. Good, maybe he will leave now, and I can escape without looking like a nervous fool.

I wish I could mold myself into the shelf because he is coming down the aisle right toward me. But, instead, I keep my head down, looking at the book in my hands, when I feel his warmth on my back. I fight the urge to melt into him when he reaches around to place a book right in front of me on the shelf.

"I think you would enjoy this one. Nice seeing you again, Dani." His breath caresses my ear before he steps away. My body misses his warmth behind me, and I have to cross my legs to fight the pulse between my thighs. Then, the door opens, and he is gone before I can gather myself. Holy Shit, this man is going to be the death of me.

I look at the book he placed in front of me, Vita Nostra, and I grab it. I don't even read the back of it; I just go to the counter to buy it because why the hell wouldn't I? Mitchell rings me up with a smile, and I rush home. I have a date with a book tonight.

Chapter Five

My mind races as I pour the small amount of water into the potted plant. I never expected to be here in this town, with people who give you a housewarming plant even though they barely know you. Miss Lenny left the plant outside with a handwritten note, "Welcome home," with care instructions attached. I still don't know how to respond to stuff like that; I've built this tough exterior as protection from everyone back home. I didn't have many friends once we moved, and everyone kind of knew me as "that bitchy quiet girl" honestly, I liked it that way. Now, I'm watering a gift from a charming stranger and staying up all night reading a book because some man recommended it to me in a way that had me sweating.

I am usually the one to leave men stumbling over their words, and there I was, stumbling over books to get a peak at the man that has me flustered for the first time. If only the convenience store guy could see me now. I roll my eyes at myself as I finish packing the leftover pizza the man so boldly left on my doorstep. It has been a long time since I've had a man make me feel this way, excited and nervous. I've had relationships before, but I've always been the more dominant one. Mainly because my feelings were never fully into any romantic relationship I had. After watching my mother's downfall, I was always scared to let anyone truly get close in case they may leave or die. This man is different; it's in the way he talks and has this confidence without being arrogant. Not to mention he is dapper and handsome in a dark, enigmatic way that has my body reacting before my brain can tell it to shut up and stop being one of those swooning pathetic females.

Moving here and starting a new life was the plan, but why can't that plan include a little romance? If he asks me out again, I'll say yes and give him a shot at messing it all up; that way, I can move on and refocus. In my experience, your idea of a man is usually much better than the actual man. So while he may seem intelligent and sexy to me now, after one date, I may find out he chews with his mouth open or ends up being a raging narcissist. Those are always fun. Although the book he recommended is excellent, I stayed up late into the night devouring half of it. So what if he has good taste in books, there has to be something wrong with him. Right?

I grab the book along with my lunch and keys and make my way out of the house. I don't have time to think about Jasper because today is my first day of work at my new job. I am so nervous but excited to start working. Mortuary science isn't for everyone, it takes a specific type of person to do this job, and I always felt a sense of pride in being one of those people. The fact that I am so emotionally detached from everything and everyone except Alex is a skill I have perfected. I don't have a long drive, so I don't even bother putting any music on in the car; I let my mind quiet itself in the silence of the vehicle before it has to sort through everything I have learned in school. I want to impress this new boss and make sure I secure my position because I really do like it here.

As I pull up to the house, my jaw drops; this is the most beautiful victorian home I have ever seen. I park by the sign saying "Cooley's Mortuary" and stand there for a second, taking it all in. The house is a two-story mammoth building that looks less like a business and more like an antique gothic home—the orange brick contrasts with the black trim and the enormous black porch. The steps leading up the porch to the front door sit off to the left while the rest of the porch wraps around the lower level of the house. This would be my dream home if I could ever afford something so extravagant. As I make my way up the steps, I start to get nervous, but I forcefully shake it off and open the front door. Here we go.

The inside of the place looks just as beautiful as the outside, with dark wood accents and a large staircase to the right. Looking to my left, I see a table of pamphlets on grief and how to deal with the loss of a loved one with a bowl of peppermints. I walk out of the entryway and into what seems to be the foyer; looking to my left, I see an open door leading to a small restroom. "Hi, you must be Danielle." The voice is moving towards me from my right, and when I turn around, I almost die. I feel my heart plummet to the very bottom of my stomach. The man that just walked out of the office to the right to greet me is standing there with his hand out, looking like he is just as stunned as I am. Before I can utter a word, I watch his shocked expression change into a devilish grin as he shakes his head. "Danielle, Dani, I should have made the connection. Well, isn't this interesting?" I don't know if he's talking to himself or me. I can't find the words to respond because this can not be happening right now. Jasper, the man who has haunted my thoughts, is standing right in front of me, and I think he is my new boss.

"What are you doing here?" I say before I can stop myself.

"Well, I live here and work here. I mean, this is my place. I'm Jasper Cooley, the owner of Cooley's Mortuary, and I appear to be your new boss." He says, looking like he can't decide if he enjoys the fact or is just as nervous as I am. Why is this happening to me?

I can not let this derail my plans; I can make this work. I mean, it's not like we had sex or anything; a little minor flirtation was all it was. I was looking for a way for him to mess up whatever was progressing, and him being my boss, has definitely done the job. This is perfect; now I can let go of whatever I thought would happen between us and refocus on the original plan.

"Well, nice to meet you again, Mr. Cooley," I say, putting my hand out to shake his, which is the professional thing to do, right?

"You can call me Jasper, I…" before he can finish, I cut him off.

"I think Mr.Cooley works just fine for me if that's alright with you." I feel my walls building faster than my thoughts can process all of this. Instead of taking the damn hint, he just gives me that smirk again, the one where the left side of his mouth tilts up just enough to cause a reaction out of me. He takes my hand in his and gives it a soft shake, his skin feels smooth, and I mentally shake the thought of his smooth hands out of my mind. Get it together, Dani.

"That's just fine with me, Danielle." He says, letting go of my hand slowly. "Let me give you the official tour of the place and show you where you can put your things. Follow me." His voice is steady and has an amused sound to it that is already getting on my nerves. How can he be so calm and amused by this? Maybe he wasn't as interested as I was the other day, and he was just being nice. That's why this isn't a big shock to him because I was the only one with romantic feelings like a dumbass. He is probably friendly to everyone he meets; that's just how the people in this town are. I mean, Miss Lenny was nice to me and even gave me a plant; I never once thought she wanted to seduce me. No, this was all in my head because he is an attractive well, dressed, well-read man, and those are rare.

He walks me down a hallway that opens up into a big kitchen with a round table off to the side. He leans against the counter and crosses his arms.

"This is the kitchen, obviously; you can put your lunch in the fridge if you need to, and there is a cabinet on the other side where you can store anything else. No one comes in here, but if you would rather store your things in my office, that's also ok." His eyes never stray from mine as he speaks. I go to the fridge and place my lunch on the top shelf. Then open the cabinet to put my bag in it, only to catch his eyes wandering once I close the small door. He doesn't make it obvious that I caught him looking at me; he just continues with his tour.

"This is my office, well, the office, I have my desk here, and I set you up one there. This is where we answer the phones and hold meetings., billing, all the administrative things an office is usually used for." He gestures to the dark room, and I peek inside. The room has one large mahogany desk in the center, while a smaller one sits off to the right. The walls are covered in shelves, and those shelves are overflowing with books. My eyes linger on a smaller shelf to the left with a record player and stacks of records underneath it. The room feels less like a business office and more like a personal office, cozy and welcoming.

"Upstairs is where I live, so we can pass that part of the tour for now." He says, and I don't miss the fact that he said for now. I shouldn't and won't be touring that upstairs part at all, Mr. Cooley, I say to myself. "Now, the real work is through here." I follow him to the side of the stairs, and behind it lies a door leading to what you would think would be a basement. He opens the door, and I follow him down several stairs until it opens into a huge room with a desk. The desk is in the center, with a computer and filing cabinets behind it. The wall to the side of the desk has a filing system hanging with manilla folders in the slots.

"This is where we document and print the reports. Everything is digital, but we print the reports and file them here. There is a restroom off to the left, and this hallway leads to the embalming room, cold storage, and the crematory." He points all this out from the desk he leans against.

"So, you just live upstairs while there is a cold storage of dead people in your basement?" I ask. I'm a little surprised by how convenient it must be to live where you work, especially when your job involves embalming the dead. He looks me in the eyes, and I try to ignore the reaction it causes.

"Well, I tell them as long as they keep the music down and clean up after themselves, I'm ok with it. Which, I haven't had any problems yet. So yeah." He smiles, and I can't help but let a small laugh escape me. This man is charming, and this is officially the worst day of my life.

"Any other questions?" He asks. Sure, I have a ton, but none that are appropriate to ask your boss.

"No, Sir. I think I'm good." I say the words, and my skin flushes as his smile fades into something else, almost predatory. He stares at me momentarily before that smile crosses his face again.

"No need to call me sir; we can keep it at Mr. Cooley or Jasper." His voice has a husky tone to it, and it makes the room feel warmer. So, he doesn't like me calling him sir?

"What's wrong with calling you, sir?" I push my luck with my question. He stops leaning against the desk and walks over to me slowly; I think he's about to walk straight into me but turns towards the hallway instead.

"We want to keep things professional, right? So let's start your training." He starts to walk down the hallway leading to the embalming room, and I release the breath I didn't even know I was holding. My skin is flushed, and I hope it doesn't show because I am almost sure I'm not reading too far into that. Calling a man sir is not unprofessional, but calling Mr. Cooley sir apparently makes him think of unprofessional thoughts. His reaction speaks volumes.

Now not only am I intrigued, but I am almost positive this will be the most challenging job I've ever had.

Chapter Six

Jasper

I have been glancing at the clock on the wall for the past ten minutes. She will be here soon, and I wish I could say I wasn't eager to see her. Why does she cause such a reaction from me; the feeling makes me uncomfortable. I have been fine on my own for a long time, but this woman is not normal. I mean that in the darkest ways, she has commanded my attention since day one without even trying. This is what I get for putting myself out there; the first woman I flirt with ends up being my new assistant. My fucking luck. I wanted the help and needed the distraction, so I guess I can't be that upset.

Let's not forget the fact that she is half my age. Since Angie had to leave me, I had given up on being with anyone else. No one else felt right after she tore my heart out and took it with her. So, dating was not even a thought until some dark, mysterious, sexy storm cloud blew into town, dropping her things in her driveway. I almost passed her up and left her to pick up her own things, but I needed to give into the gravitational pull her ass was giving me. God, that sounds so horrible when I admit it to myself, but it's no worse than the thoughts that ran through my head yesterday. The minute the word Sir left those plump lips, the thought of her crawling across the floor to me, begging, invaded my vision.

The front door opens and closes, and I wait to see her fill the doorway to my office, our office. I have to push out these thoughts because I am her boss now, and the last thing I need is to ruin the business I've worked my whole life to build. The business I have killed to have, and I won't let anything screw that up. I'm reading her body language all wrong; she can't be attracted to me. Women like that don't like older men like me. I lost count of the number of grey strands that's invaded my hair, and although I'm in good shape, I'm sure she wants a young man her age. Fuck, why am I even thinking about this? She is your assistant Jasper, that's it! You need her to keep you in check, to help out. You need her. Get it together, and stop being some horny old man.

"Good Morning. I brought you this. I hope you take it black." She hands me a cup of coffee and smiles nervously. The previous thought process goes right out the fucking window, and I am sad to admit I may just be a horny old man because, damn it, she looks beautiful.

"Thanks, you didn't have to do that," I say. I can tell she wants to say more, but she looks around the office before her eyes settle back on mine.

"Look, I may be way off here, and I hope I don't offend you. But I just wanted to say that I hope this isn't weird or awkward, and we can maybe just move past the other day. I mean with the whole pizza thing, which was really sweet, by the way, and…I just don't want you to feel weird around me. I guess what I mean is.." She stumbles over her words, and I'm trying not to smile. She is talking about the pizza she didn't throw out because I saw her eating the leftovers yesterday in the kitchen and reading the book I recommended, although she quickly pushed it aside when I walked in like she wasn't reading it. I didn't say anything; I just left her to her lunch and book, but a part of me warmed knowing she didn't throw it out. She stops talking and takes a deep breath.

"Sorry, I meant to say I hope we can work together professionally and forget that you asked me on a lunch date. Before we knew we would be working together. I mean, I'm sure you were just being nice, but just in case, I don't want any weirdness between us. Am I still rambling? I'm just going to shut up now." She says with a small smile and shakes her head. I like seeing her nervous. I have a feeling she isn't usually this nervous, she has an air about her that is so dominating, but she's all nerves when she speaks to me.

"I am not offended at all. I was just being friendly. Let's get to work." I won't explain more than that because I'm an asshole, and I like seeing the way she bites her lower lip and rolls her eyes at herself. Yeah, she isn't used to this at all. I can picture the men she's been with before bending to her every word and kissing her ass. That's not me; it never was. I like to be in control, especially when it comes to sex. My sexual tastes aren't for everyone, and while I think Danielle would make a perfect little brat, I have to remind myself that she's my assistant, and this whole thing would only be complicated. Not to mention, I haven't been with anyone in so long.

"That's it?" she asks as I walk past her to get the day started. She wanted some explanation. She wanted me to tell her she was reading this all wrong and apologize for asking her on a lunch date. I can't do that because if she weren't my assistant, I would have asked her on another date. What I can do is respect her wishes to keep this professional because I agree we need to work together and not get wrapped up in whatever this is.

I stop in the doorway, taking a sip of the coffee she brought me, some kind of peace offering to soften the blow she thought she was about to deliver.

"Yeah, that's it. Don't make it weird, Danielle. We have work to do." I say with a smart-ass smile that I know she picks up on because before I turn to walk out, I see her narrow her eyes at me.

"Sure, well, I just wanted to clear up any confusion." I hear her say behind me as she follows me downstairs. I was impressed with her yesterday; she quickly picked up on things, and I can honestly say she will make a good assistant. Lord knows I've needed the help for a long time. Having Danielle here will keep me in check and give me some time away from the bodies. I've been alone with them too long.

"No confusion here, Danielle. We are here to do a job. That's all I expect from you." I say, letting her know I'm done with the conversation. Although I won't say it out loud, she is right, and I need to respect the fact that she wants to keep this all professional. I mean, she's acting like we had sex or something; I flirted and asked her out on a date, that's it. We can move past that and do our jobs. I will have to make a mental note not to push her buttons, no matter how adorable she is when she's nervous. The downstairs office area always greets you with a chill in the air. Moving to the desk, I busy myself with papers as she follows.

"Great. Well, are we starting on Mrs. Bergeron?" She says as she pulls the embalming folder off the desk and reads the name. She is back to business with a stern look on her face. Yesterday, I let her follow me through many of the procedures, but she picked up so quickly I want to test her out on her own today. A guilty part of me wants to make her nervous again, but I believe she knows what she's doing.

"You will be starting on Mrs. Bergeron today; I will be assisting," I say without looking up from the report I'm printing. I can hear her close the folder and shuffle her feet.

"Wait, by myself. Already?" She sounds excited, but I can hear the faint sound of her anxiety.

"You did very well yesterday, and I want to see how well you do taking the lead. Eventually, I will need you ready to take callouts, and I believe you are knowledgeable enough to handle that. So, today I will be observing mostly." I finally look at her, and she has a massive smile on her face, and it catches me off guard. She is such a serious woman, so her smile can take your breath away. She's beautiful in this dark, classic way that I can appreciate, and I try not to stare.

"Show me what you got," I say, handing her the report to put in the folder. She takes it and softens her smile. I can tell she likes that I trust her to take the lead. She doesn't say anything; she just turns around and leads the way into the embalming room. I try to keep my eyes off her ass as it sways back and forth down the long hallway between the office and the embalming room. She has to be doing that on purpose; no one sways their hips like that naturally; the way her ass bounces slightly in her black pants has me slightly hypnotized.

She walks into the cold embalming room and starts setting up her station as I watch from the doorway. I watch her move effortlessly around the room like she's been here for years. She knows where everything is, stopping only briefly to remember the exact spots. She doesn't even glance my way, the nerves I thought were there disappear, and she is in this focused state of mind that has me smiling.

"So, if it is ok with you, I'd like you to talk through your process, and I'll ask questions as we go." I let her know what I expect and lean against the counter. She finally looks at me and nods her head.

"Ok, the first thing I did was set up my station, and now I will go to cold storage to retrieve the body." She says as I follow her lead through the swinging doors leading down another long hallway to cold storage.

"I will double-check the name on the report and the body, and then I will move her to the embalming room once verified." She says as she finds the name and pulls Mrs. Bergeron out and onto the gurney.

"Why do we double-check the name, and what would you do if they didn't match?" I ask a question I know she knows the answer to. I just want to hear her voice as it echoes around the silent room. She looks over her shoulder as she pushes Mrs. Bergeron down the hall.

"Well, we double-check to make sure we have the right report, right body. If they don't match, I will update the file." She answers in a matter-of-fact tone and finishes settling Mrs. Bergeron in the embalming room.

"Very good. Now, take me through your steps." I say, taking a mental note of how she reacts to my praise. She smiles briefly but is back to her stern demeanor quickly.

"First, I will inspect the body for identifying marks and injuries if any are present." She doesn't wait for me to tell her she's correct; she just moves. She doesn't flinch at all when lifting Mrs. Bergeron's stiff arm; she flows like a well-oiled machine through the process.

Once she's done, I look over her report and the body, giving her my approval once I see she hasn't missed anything. If she is nervous, I can not tell; she waited patiently for me to look everything over with a sense of knowing she didn't miss a thing.

"Perfect, I agree with your report. You're doing very well. What's next?" I place the report in the folder and glance briefly to see that smile again. You will miss it if you wait too long, but I'm glad I didn't.

"I will mix the embalming fluid." She rubs her hands together and moves to get the fluids. She starts pouring the methanol into the machine, and I move closer to watch. I can smell the faint smell of cinnamon from her perfume over the methanol as

I pass behind her. She reaches for the formaldehyde and starts pouring again, only then taking notice of me standing there.

"Why do we use formaldehyde?" I ask another question to break the silence. She knows what I'm doing and looks at me as she pours.

"It's used for firming and preserving the tissue. I used the methanol to hold the formaldehyde in the solution, preventing polymerization. I'll also mix in glutaraldehyde, and once the mixture is complete, I'll make my incision in the carotid artery and jugular vein with the scalpel and forceps. Then I'll clamp the tubing to both veins and connect the embalming pump." She answers with a smirk showing me just how knowledgeable she is, and fuck; I'm in trouble.

Angie never took an interest in my work; it freaked her out. Until one day, she came poking around in here, and I wish she would have never even tried. So, I've never had another woman in this room touching my tools and doing my job so effortlessly. I had no idea this would be so goddamn arousing. She is intelligent and gorgeous, and I can watch her work all day. I don't hide the smile on my face, and when she looks back at me, only then do I see her get nervous.

"What?" She asks, pausing for a moment.

"Nothing, I'm just very impressed. You would swear you've worked here for years." I grab the forceps and the scalpel for her and stand beside her. I hand her the scalpel first, and she takes it with a smile.

She places her hand on the body, and it's the first time I see her wince slightly. She makes the incision smoothly, and I hand her the forceps.

"I never get used to how cold they are." She says, letting me know why she showed the briefest discomfort. I know she can feel my eyes watching her, and I try to keep my arousal out of my expression. The last thing I need is to get turned on by her in front of a dead body, she would turn in her resignation by the afternoon, and I wouldn't blame her.

"Well, if it makes you feel any better. I knew Mrs. Bergeron before she died, and I can assure you she was just as cold alive as she is now" I hand her the forceps, and she takes them, moving quickly but now more relaxed. She works quietly for a moment, and I hope I didn't offend her.

"Sorry, you develop a dark sense of humor when you've been doing this for as long as I have. I meant no disrespect to the dead." I explain as I watch her clamp the tubing.

"No, it's fine. I don't mind. I personally have always been fascinated with death. Death seems easy in comparison to life. Life is what's hard. Life causes wounds that take years to heal; death heals them instantly. There is something both terrifying and lovely in the finality of it all. ...Sorry, that sounds pretty bad." She speaks as she works. Once finished, she puts her hands on her hips and looks over what she's done.

Her words touch a part of me that has me mesmerized by her. She's young but wise, which tells me she knows pain. She's felt the pain of losing a loved one, and it is felt in her words.

"No, it's quite beautiful, actually," I say, trying to hide the gravel in my tone, and out of habit, I reach over to turn on the embalming pump. She does the same, and our hands meet on the button, but neither of us pulls it away. Instead, like a sappy romance novel, we linger briefly in each other's touch. Her skin is soft and warm, a stark contrast to the body we have been working on.

Pulling her hand back, she smiles, "Not used to someone else leading." I can hear the challenge in her voice.

"No, not at all. Sorry, I just moved out of habit." I try to play off what I know we both felt, but I don't move away from her side.

"Yeah, or you were just trying to hold my hand." She teases with an eye roll.

I hear my brain telling me to stop, but my body doesn't listen as I take a step closer, but before I can say anything, we both are startled. Dani grabs my arms as she jumps from the sound, and I love feeling her this close, but what the fuck is that? Loud music starts blaring from upstairs.

"Sorry, I'll go check on that," I say, pushing her softly out of my arms to check on the sound coming from upstairs. As I climb the stairs, the music gets louder; it's coming from the office. I step inside and see the record player is on, and once I stop to recognize the song, I quickly take it off. I look around the office and all of upstairs when I hear Dani yell, "Everything ok?"

I don't see anyone, so I yell back that everything is fine and return to the office. I go back to the record player and reach behind it to unplug it. I don't want to ever have to hear that song again. That was her favorite song, and she's gone now.

Chapter Seven

Dani

Pairing my black dress pants with a gray sweater, I take one final look In the mirror. I'm tempted to wipe off the lipstick I put on, but I decide against it. I'm lying to myself if I say I don't want to get a reaction out of Jasper. The sexual tension is insane, and I know I should be doing everything to keep this professional; there is just something about this man that makes me angry and turned on simultaneously. I thought I would walk into the office yesterday and, put my foot down, lay down some boundaries. Then I was the first one to cross that boundary. If we don't act on the tension, then we are doing nothing wrong. A little harmless flirting won't hurt anything.

I roll my eyes a the thought because I already know I'm screwed in this situation, but I am determined to make this work. I decide to call and check on Alex before I back out of the driveway to head into another day of dead bodies and trying not to tempt my boss into bending me over the desk. This wouldn't be my life if it wasn't weird and fucked up, though, so I should be able to handle this.

"Hey, Loser," Alex answers after a few rings, and his voice sends a jolt through me. I miss him so much that it hurts.

"You should be getting ready for school. Are you getting ready?" I try to take my emotions out of my voice.

"Geez, yes, I'm going to be leaving in five. How's the job? You like it?" He asks, and the job is the last thing on my mind. I don't want to tell him how great everything is here because he should be here now.

"Well, it's a job. I like it, but I'm calling to check on you. I don't want to talk about myself. How is everything there? You still have the money?" I ask, not caring that I am attacking him with questions this early in the morning. I don't miss the fact that he pauses for a moment, and my pulse starts to pick up.

"I still have the money." He says, avoiding my other question.

"Ok, and how is everything there? Why do I feel like you're not telling me something?" My ears flush with heat, waiting for him to tell me something that will piss me off.

"Look, it's nothing, Dani, everything is ok. I can handle it. You are coming to get me in a month, right? So, stop worrying. I got to head to school." Alex tries to rush me off the phone.

"Alex, damn it, just tell me what's going on, or I'm driving back to find out for myself." I know something is happening, and I'm not getting off this phone until he tells me.

"Please, just don't freak out. I promise I can handle it." He says, and now I'm really about to freak out.

"Fine, I'll be there in a few hours," I say.

"God, Dani, fine, Craig is back. Ok? He hasn't even tried to talk to me. Mom and him have been high most of the time anyway; I doubt they even remember I live here. Just don't freak out. I'll spend the night at Nick's house if I see that he might get out of control. I can handle this. "He urges me not to freak out, but every cell in my body is set on fire. Of course, she would let Craig back once I moved out. I bet she couldn't wait until I even left the driveway.

"Since when? How long has he been there?" I ask, but I know the answer.

"The day after you left, I came home to him and mom laughing in the bedroom. I knew it was him, so I went straight to my room. He comes and goes but hasn't said anything to me. I'm sorry, Dani. Please don't come home right now. You don't need to be around him, and I don't want you to mess up anything you have going on out there. You are my ticket out of this shit hole. So trust me, please. I got this." His words tear me apart, and I fight back the tears.

"Fine, but the minute he even raises his voice to you, get the fuck out of there. Go to Nick's, go anywhere, and call me immediately. I'll drop everything and come pick you up, you know that. I don't know if I can relax knowing he is there. Maybe I should just come to get you. Fuck it. It may put you behind, but I'd rather you be safe." I want to scream, but I know it won't help. No matter how loud I made my voice, it was never heard; she never heard me. She never heard me when I told her how he would grope me in the kitchen when I was trying to cook dinner. Dinner that she never cooked because she was too wasted to stand at the stove. She never heard me when I yelled for her at the top of my lungs while he let himself into my room in the middle of the night. She never heard me, and she never will.

"It's ok. I love you. Let's stick to the plan, and I'll be fine. I've learned the signs of when they get out of control. Don't worry about me. I'll call if anything happens, you know that. Now, go to work, bum. I have to go to school." He assures me he will be ok, and we say our goodbyes.

I can feel my blood boiling under my skin, and I have to take several breaths to calm the anger brewing inside of me. How could she be so heartless? So stupid? Driving to work isn't enough time to clear my head. When I park the car, I slam the door without noticing how hard I slammed it. The sound pulls me back, and I need to focus. I hate to admit he's right, It's up to me to make this work here so I can get him, and we can both leave that town in the rearview mirror and never look back. We were never meant to rot there with her, and dad would have wanted us to get as far away as possible.

I soften my expression as I open the door and step inside to start the day. I want to throw myself into today's work and distract myself from the worry coursing through my body. I know every day Alex is in that house with them is a risk, and I don't think I can wait much longer. I'll give myself until the end of today to devise a plan to get him sooner.

"Good Morning" Jasper passes me on the way to the kitchen as I follow him to put my things down. I forget to hide the book from him as I place it on the counter to open the fridge.

"How's the book?" He asks as he pours a cup of coffee from the pot he must have just made. The kitchen smells just as good as the coffee shop, and I am dying for a cup. I was hoping he didn't notice that I actually bought the book but seeing how I can't put it down; I figured I'd take the risk of him seeing it.

"I'm enjoying it and have about 40 pages left." I don't mean to be short with him; I know my situation isn't his fault. He has been friendly to me, and is why I can make a life out here. I am grateful he even took a chance on a newly graduated woman with minimal previous experience.

"Just enjoying it?" he takes a sip from his mug and leans against the counter. I feel like he can pick up on my mood and is trying to make me talk. I wish I could say I can resist, but I feel the urge to talk to him; I'm surprised by the desire to spill my guts to him about everything that's going on. I barely know this man, but I want to tell him everything. It must be black magic, that's it; he is some voodoo practitioner and is breaking down my walls with his spellbinding charm. Fuck, I am losing my mind.

"Ok, fine. I love it. It's a much darker, stranger, and more menacing version of Hogwarts. The setting alone makes the book amazing." I answer his question, and how his eyes light up at my answer makes me smile. He is so proud of himself, and it shows.

"Right, that's the vibe I was getting as well. I loved Sasha; she was great. I have more recommendations if you ever need some. And vice versa, I'd love to take any suggestions from you. I keep a lot of my books in the office; if you ever want to borrow one, you are welcome to it. Call it a perk of the job." He says, sipping from his mug again.

"I may have to take you up on that offer. Although I have a stack at home, I still need to get to. Thanks though; that's really trusting of you. I can't say I trust anyone to borrow my books." I say, closing the cabinets and leaning against the counter across from him.

"Well, I'd just hold your paycheck till you bring it back." He says with a small laugh. This is nice, and I don't want to stop talking to him, which scares me because he makes talking to him so easy. My phone buzzes in my pocket; pulling it out, I see it's Alex.

Alex: Hey, I just wanted to let you know I love you. I know you're worried, and I appreciate everything you're doing. I'm sorry about this morning. I didn't want to worry you before work. Just chill and know that this will all be over soon. I'm sure dad would be proud. Love you, Loser.

My throat burns with the tears I'm holding back. I can feel Jasper's eyes on me, and the last thing I need is for him to see me crying at work. I take a big breath and busy myself with finding a mug.

"You want to talk about it?" He asks, and his question stops me for a moment. Why would he care? He probably doesn't want me bringing my drama to work.

"It's nothing. Just family stuff. It won't affect my work." I assure him as I find a mug and start pouring.

"I'm not worried about it affecting your work, Dani; it's not like we work with people that can complain. I'm asking because I know you're alone out here, and if you need someone to talk to, I'm here." He says Dani instead of Danielle, and it only makes me feel how personal he is trying to be. He wants me to know this isn't him talking to me as my boss but as something more.

"Is that another perk of the job?" I say, taking that first sip of coffee that touches your soul.

"No, that's a bonus, smart ass." He teases, and my ears have that familiar flush of heat. But, this time, it's not anger that has them warm; instead, it's this gorgeous man that is breaking down my barriers no matter how much I want to try and keep them up.

"I just have a lot going on back at home, well, back where I moved from. I left someone behind, and I miss them very much." I want to take back the words before I say them because I know confiding in him is crossing a line.

"Oh, I see. That boyfriend you mentioned. The Poe fan." He crosses his arms, trying not to look disappointed, but I can see it on his face. Part of me wants to let him keep thinking I have some boyfriend Im pining for back home. The look on his face has me feeling things I shouldn't, and I let him sit with that thought for a little.

"My brother. He's fifteen, and I've practically raised him. Our mom is …well, she's unstable. I moved out here to start a new life, and I plan on bringing him here soon. I just wanted to establish us here before uprooting him from school. I hate leaving him there. I feel guilty being here while he deals with everything back there." I watch him look both relieved and empathetic at the same time.

"Don't feel guilty; the world beats us up enough, and we don't need to beat ourselves up as well. I'm sure your brother is very grateful to have you." He says.

"Yeah, I guess you're right," I shrug. His expression changes, and instead of looking at me, I feel like he's looking inside me. That devilish grin is back and is setting my skin on fire.

"Of course I am." He teases. "You're a strong woman Dani; you know that?" His teasing tone changes into a sound of appreciation, and I melt. I have to disagree because if he knew how weak I was to his words and that smirk, he would know I'm far from strong when it comes to him. I can't help the soft smile I feel tugging the corners of my mouth. He sets down the cup and moves closer. I look down into my cup because his presence is intoxicating. I feel his fingers hook under my chin and tilt my head up to meet his eyes. This is the first time he touches me, and damn, it feels good.

"And you're beautiful and smart." His words feel like they drift across my skin like the soft caress of a lover's hands.

"Let me take you to dinner tonight." His offer shakes me out of the trance he has me in.

"You know we can't do this. You're my boss, Jasper, and I'm complicated." I say, pushing his hand away gently to finish picking up my things.

"So, I'll just leave takeout on your front porch again, got it." He says with a smile. He doesn't let my denial deter him or embarrass him. The man exudes a confidence that makes me cut my eyes at him.

"Ok, Ok, just a joke." He puts his hands up with that same smile, and I'm grateful he doesn't make this awkward. He has a way of turning my denial into a line he toys with, poking at it with the tip of his shoe. I laugh at his words because one day, I know I'll end up letting him cross that line. The thought scares me but also heats me to my core. I make sure he is turning to walk out of the kitchen before I clench my thighs a little tighter. "Hang in there, girl," I whisper to the part of me that is having the hardest time respecting that line.

Chapter Eight

Jasper

The soft clink of the ice hitting the bottom of the glass fills the quiet room. Pouring the Bourbon over it, I let my mind wander. My mind doesn't have to wander far; Dani is always there to occupy it. It's been four days since I touched her in the kitchen. My fingers still feel the warmth of her skin against them as I rub them together. I don't know what made me cross that line, but my body sometimes has a mind of its own. She has been doing well despite having the personal issues she's dealing with. She dives into her work, and I can't help but to stop and watch her sometimes. The way she wrinkles her nose just a bit when first putting her hands on the bodies. My favorite thing is how her pale skin flushes when she notices I'm watching, yet her eyes are still set on her task.

Taking a sip, the Bourbon warms my chest as I sit down with my book. I open the page I left off on but stare at the words because my mind isn't finished with her yet. I know she has a lot going on outside of work, and I should back off. For the most part, I have. My body betrays me when I catch myself staring at the fine angles of her jaw or when I move just a little closer to catch the soft scent of her perfume. I'm, of course, discreet about it because I don't want to pressure her or make her feel weird. Her mind is so busy with work and her troubles that she doesn't notice much.

I knew she had a mature way about her, but I didn't think it was because she had no choice but to be that way. Raising her brother and going as far as to move away and start a new life for both of them is such a tough thing to do, especially at her age. She's in her twenties but is forced to settle down and create a home for herself and her brother. I say forced, but I feel like she doesn't feel forced at all. She seems to take pride in being there for her brother, and it's admirable. Which makes it that much harder for me not to want to take care of her; sure, she takes care of her brother but who is there to take care of her? To rub her feet after a long day, to cook her a nice meal so she can relax with a glass of wine, I feel the urge to do these things for her, and I know I shouldn't. She was just supposed to be my assistant. Someone to help take part of the workload so I can distance myself from my work.

Any other man would consider her situation as baggage and not worth the trouble, but something in me only pulls me closer. I want to alleviate the stress of living her day-to-day life. I wonder how bad off her mother is that she can't take care of them. She said she was unstable, but I didn't press further to determine what she meant by unstable. Is her health unstable? Her mental health? It must be bad if she feels she needs to take her brother and herself as far away as she can from it.

Angie and I wanted kids, but it just never happened. That was the beginning of our downfall when I couldn't give her children. I guess a higher power knew she wouldn't be sticking around. The thought of her has me downing the rest of the Bourbon and placing it on the table next to me. My whole world shattered when she had to leave, and I never once thought I could begin to put the pieces back together again. The thought of her still stings, but I notice it doesn't sting as much tonight. I can't expect Dani to pick up the shattered pieces, but having her here each day does make me feel like the pieces are all swept up into one pile. I don't feel so scattered; I feel a sense of excitement having her here but also a sense of peace. She quiets the loud thoughts that have been yelling in the back of my mind for years.

My phone rings; pulling it out, I see who it is and sigh in frustration. Of course, I get a call out the night I decide to have a few drinks. I should have known this because callouts are common in my work. Unfortunately, the grim reaper doesn't take vacation days. The now three glasses of Bourbon have me trying extra hard to concentrate on the voice on the other end of the phone. Hanging up, I realize I have about thirty minutes to get my shit together because I have two bodies coming in. Then the thought hits me, and I am suddenly not too upset about this call out. Pulling up her number, I call Dani and wait for her to pick up while trying to hide my enthusiasm. When she answers, I stand up and pace the room.

"So, I have a call out for you if possible. I um….. it's two bodies…I could use the help. If you're not…ummm. You know, busy or anything." I try not to stumble on my words, hoping she doesn't notice.

"Are you ok?" she asks, and I realize that she has, in fact, noticed.

"Well, I have had a few drinks. I'm not drunk or anything. Just a slight buzz, but if you can't come, that's totally understandable." I try not to sound like a drunken fool. I'm not drunk, just a little warm and tingly, which could be the liquor, or it could be her voice causing this reaction. Who knows?

"I'll be right over." She says with a hint of laughter and hangs up before I can thank her. I instantly go into the bathroom to brush my teeth and freshen up. I don't want to smell like Bourbon or look like a mess. Staring at my reflection, I try not to let self-doubt creep in. Dani and I are getting along well but would someone as beautiful as that woman really be into a guy like me? Turning my head from side to side, I take one last appraising look. I'm a handsome guy, sure I'm a little up there in age, but it adds to the charm. Right?

I give myself a wink in the mirror, then instantly regret it. Yep, I'm a cheesy old man, and Dani could do so much better. I start to head downstairs to prepare for the drop-off. Dani should be here soon, so I start to get things ready. As I'm preparing reports, the door opens, and it's like my body knows she's here before my eyes can see her.

"In here," I call out from the office so she doesn't go downstairs. She walks in, and I have to remind myself not to stare. Her hair is drawn back in a low bun at the base of her neck, and I want to trail kisses up the exposed sides so badly. As usual, she wears black dress pants with a black button-down shirt partly tucked in. The top of the shirt hangs slightly lower on one side, exposing even more skin I want to touch.

"So, are they already here?" She asks while throwing on a grey sweater that somehow still makes her look so put together and sexy.

"No," I say, not explaining further. She gives me a questioning look.

"Are they on the way?" She asks, coming closer to the desk. I don't know if the liquor is making everything around her blurry or if I am just that intoxicated at the sight of her, but I don't answer.

"Or maybe they aren't coming at all, and this is your way of getting me here." She teases.

"If I said they weren't coming, and this was all just a way to get you here with me, would you stay?" I ask, watching for a reaction.

"I'd say that callouts are for actual callouts, and that's cheating to use them to get me here so late at night. What's that called an abuse of power?" She comes around the desk and leans on the side crossing her arms.

"So you're saying I have power over you?" I ask while closing the distance between us, pausing only to make sure she doesn't mind. Her eyes lock onto mine, and she bites that damn lip again. The tension in the room is thick, and we both know there is no longer any way of denying it. She uncrosses her arms and leans back against the desk to face me; I want to lay her down across it and explore her beautiful body. Instead, I run my fingers across the smooth skin of her neck, hooking my fingers under her chin while using my thumb to pull her bottom lip from her teeth.

"Unfortunately, I'm afraid you do." Her words have taken on a raspy tone that makes my dick twitch. I lean in closer, my lips barely brushing hers when the loud knock at the door comes.

"Let's get to work,'" My words fall across her lips like a soft breath, and I slowly back away and gesture for her to leave the room first. "Ladies first, of course."

She looks at me in a daze realizing this was actually a call out. She smiles and rolls her eyes before walking out before me, and I make sure to adjust myself before answering the door. I swing open the door expecting to see that the bodies have arrived, but instead, I stare out at an empty porch. Stepping out, I walk to the side, looking to see if they went around back, but I see no one. Then the headlights pull into the driveway, and I recognize the van; the bodies are just getting here. So, who was banging on the door?

Confused, I help unload the bodies and thank them for coming. Dani seems to have gathered herself up nicely and is in that familiar "work" mode that I admire so much. We get to work on the bodies, and I forget all about the odd knocking at the door. We don't have a lot of kids in town, so the odds of it being some prank are slim but not impossible. I brush it off and finish the work in less time than usual now that Dani is here to help. To think I used to do this alone, now I don't know if I could. She has spoiled me to having help, and I hope she never leaves.

"Here's my report on Feilds," She says, handing me the folder to file. I reach for it as she pulls it away, teasing. She smiles, giving it to me again, only to pull it away the minute I reach for it.

"Are you done?" I say, acting like I'm not enjoying her little game.

"Oh, I'm sorry. I thought you still wanted to play." She teases before handing it to me. I smile, not grabbing for it immediately. She stares back innocently, her eyes saying I could take it, but I know better. She sees me reaching for it, and before she can pull it back again, I grab her hand instead, pulling her into me. She falls right into my kiss, and I swear the world fucking stops. Our lips pressed together for a moment before we both silently agreed that this is happening. Dropping the folder, she links her hands behind my head and relaxes into my kiss.

Her lips are soft, and she parts them slightly, allowing my tongue to slip in. I feel almost dizzy kissing her; I've imagined this moment since the day I met her. I asked myself many times how sweet her kiss would be. Her kiss is even sweeter than I imagined, and my body feels alive for the first time in a long time. I pull away from our kiss only to trail more down her jawline, to her ear, and down her neck, as I feel her run her fingers through my hair, almost guiding my lips to where she wants them. Running my hands down the soft curves of her body, I hook my hands behind her knees and lift her onto the desk.

BANG, BANG, BANG BANG

A series of loud knocks banging on the door upstairs has us pulling away and Dani hopping off the desk.

"Jesus, have they been knocking?" She wipes her lips and adjusts her clothes. I adjust myself for the second time tonight, and before I can walk off, I hear her giggle.

"Come here." She pulls me in and smooths out my hair which she must have messed up. She smiles and places a soft kiss on my lips. My heart does this flutter that lets me know I'm in trouble. She thinks I have power over her, but she has no idea.

BANG, BANG, BANG BANG

"Give me a second!" I call up as I make my way up the stairs. This better be an emergency with how they are about to break down my front door.

BANG BANG BANG

I watch the door rattle with the loud knocking as I approach it. Swinging it open, furious, I'm greeted with the sight of..no one. Quickly stepping out onto the porch, rushing to the side, and looking out into the yard, I still see no one. The night is dark and quiet; not even a rustle of leaves can be heard. The door slams behind me, and I cringe at the sound. I hurry back and open it to see Dani coming up from downstairs. She couldn't have closed this. Two options crossed my mind: either the wind was suddenly strong, or we may have a ghost. I laugh at the thought. I have dealt with dead bodies my entire career, and none have come to haunt me. Another thought crosses my mind, but I push it away quickly as I feel a chill crawl down my spine.

"Everything ok? Who was that?" Dani asks, stopping by the stairs.

"No one. Probably some kids were playing around." I assure her, although she doesn't look like she believes me.

"That happens often around here?" She asks.

"Not really, but I can't think of anything else it could be," I say, words I'm not sure I believe either.

"Well, maybe I should get going." She says nervously, like she isn't sure I want to pick up where we left off. I pull her into my arms and kiss her softly. When I pull away, she stares into my eyes.

"I can't believe you took a call out only so you can come to take advantage of me. Seducing me when you knew I was drunk." I tease and laugh at her expression as her mouth falls open.

"Oh, shut up! You were not drunk, and you seduced me, sir." She says, smacking my arm playfully.

"There's that word again. Sir." placing soft kisses along her neck again, I can't stop touching her.

"Oh, that's true. You like that word, don't you? Sir.." She challenges me, and I swear I feel all the blood in my body rush straight to my dick. I start to suck and nip at the creamy skin of her neck and only move lower when she releases a moan that is like fucking music to my ears.

When the sound of a phone ringing cuts through the silent room, we both groan in frustration.

"Sorry, I have to get that." She rushes into the office to answer her phone. I'm standing at the base of the stairs looking down at my dick, who I am sure hates me right now. So when I hear her start to yell from the office, my dick is the last thing on my mind.

"What the fuck do you mean he hit you! I'm going to fucking kill him! Where are you? I'm coming right now! Stay there." She yells into the phone as I stand in the office doorway. She is pacing like a caged animal, and she is almost scary.

"Hey, hey, what's going on?" I try to calm her down, but it doesn't work.

"I need to go; I have to go get my brother. That piece of shit put his hands on him. I wasn't there! I should have been there. Alex should have been here. I fucked up." She is rambling, and the tears are starting to fall.

"Let me drive you there. Come on, let's go." I start to grab her things to carry out to my car.

"No, I shouldn't involve you. I'm sorry I can handle this. I should have handled this." She says, but I don't listen; I just usher her out onto the porch.

"Jasper, give me my things." She says, reaching.

"Stop. You're in no shape to drive, and I won't argue, so get your ass in the car and let me take you." I open the passenger door, and she doesn't argue; she just hops in. Before I can turn the key in the ignition, her tears start flowing.

"I'm going to kill him." She says, and I can feel her rage fill the car. I don't say anything; I just reach across and grab her hand. She looks down at our hands but doesn't pull away.

"Just give me the address, and I'll get you there. You're not dealing with all this heavy shit on your own anymore. Understand?" I look into her eyes, and I feel like wrapping my hands around the throat of whoever caused her this much pain. She blinks away more tears and gives me the address.

The GPS says we have three hours to make it there, but I'll try and make it there faster. She doesn't let go of my hand but leans back against the headrest and stares out the window. I make a mental note right then and there that I never want to have to see her cry like this again.

Chapter Nine

Dani

My mind is on fire, an anger I haven't felt in a very long time. Guilt, rage, and fear are all fighting to take over, and I'm trying not to lose it. When Alex told me Craig was back in the house, I should have gone to get him. I can't believe she let him back in after everything that has happened. Now, my boss is driving me three hours away to pick up Alex, and this is so fucked up. I feel Jasper looking over every few minutes to silently check on me, rubbing my hand softly with his thumb. Yes, he is my boss, but I know things have changed after that kiss tonight. Even though lines have been crossed, I would never have wanted to drag him into my bullshit. I'm sure he will have no problem keeping our relationship professional after tonight. What grown man would want to deal with all of this baggage? I'm a fucking basket case, and I'm sure he is only driving me there because that's just the type of man he is. Jasper is a gentleman, caring and thoughtful.

"You ready to tell me what's going on?" Jasper's voice pulls my attention from the blurring trees outside the window. Since he is driving all this way, I should at least let him know what he is walking into.

"I have to go get my brother sooner than expected, which is fine because I have been worried about him since our conversation the other day. Unfortunately, my mom's boyfriend moved back in." I can barely say the last few words. The anger I have for that woman is not something any daughter should have to feel for her mother.

"Ok, so your brother and the boyfriend don't get along?" He asks.

"Alex is a good kid; he's not some kid rebelling against his mom's new boyfriend. It's nothing like that. This guy, Craig, is a piece of shit. And despite what he's done to me, to us, my mom moved him back in the minute I left." I say, fighting the tears that are threatening to fall again.

"What do you mean what he's done to you? He's abusive?" he asks, and I see how his body tenses at the thought. I don't know why I'm telling him all of this. I know he is just trying to make conversation but spilling my trauma is not something I want to do. Especially when it will only push him further away; my thoughts flash back to just over an hour ago when his lips were on mine, and I can almost feel them there again. I was stupid to think my past wouldn't come pulling me back the minute I felt an ounce of happiness.

"It doesn't matter. I just need to get Alex. You didn't have to do this, by the way. I could have driven." I let go of his hand and mess with an imaginary piece of dust on my pants. I can feel his eyes on me then, as if he is angry that I pulled away; he reaches and grabs my hand back.

"Yes, it does fucking matter, Dani. I know you are dealing with some things on your own, some heavy things. I want to lighten that load, and if that means being someone you can talk to, then we have another hour for you to get whatever you need off your chest." His voice is stern, but the feelings behind his words are warm, and I want to fall into them. I want to tell him everything, but I'm scared. Sensing my hesitation, he pulls my hand up and kisses it softly. I feel my body relax, but I know after tonight, whatever feelings he thinks he has for me will be gone. I decide to enjoy this while I can.

"Yes, he was abusive. This is the first time he has actually hit Alex. Before, he would just push him around. I was the one who took most of the abuse." My words taste like vomit as they spill out, and I don't feel like I can stop them even though I feel his hand tighten just a little in mine.

"At first, my mom and him would just get high and drunk and leave us alone. Then once she let him move in, he realized that she would pass out, which would make him switch his attention to me. He started by groping me in the kitchen or when I passed through the hall. He would push his body against mine or rub a hand across me." The words I've never told anyone besides my mom are flowing along with the tears, and I can't stop. My mind is telling me to shut up, but for the first time, I feel like someone is actually hearing me.

"I told my mom about it. She got irate and confronted him. He denied everything, of course, and said it was me that was coming onto him. They started yelling, and I was told to go to my room. I could hear them screaming back and forth, and I thought for sure my mom was going to protect me. Then the next morning, he sat at the kitchen table with a smile that told me he got away with it. She wasn't going to kick him out." I stop to collect myself because that morning has replayed in my mind so many times. She didn't know it, but she gave him power that day.

"So, a few days later, I woke up in the middle of the night to him standing beside my bed. He told me that if I tried to tell my mom, she wouldn't believe me. All he had to do was dangle that little baggy in front of her face, and she believed every word out of his mouth. He said no one would believe me because they would think I was just like my mom. A whore who wanted it. I tried to fight him off of me, I screamed and screamed, but she never came. It was Alex who busted into the room and went to wake her up. By then, he was off of me and running after Alex to explain himself to my mom. He said I called him to my room, and he was sorry he gave in to me. He blamed me for everything. She kicked him out that night, but she blamed me too. She didn't believe it wasn't my fault when I said he raped me. She just kept yelling at me that it's my fault, and I wanted to split them up." I can't control the tears as the words fall out of my mouth. I feel him let go of my hand, and the car veers off the road and comes to a stop.

I try to blink away the tears to see what he is doing. I watch through blurry eyes as he comes around the front of the car and opens my door. Leaning over, he unbuckles my seatbelt.

"Come here." He says as he pulls me out of the car and into his body. In the middle of nowhere on the side of the road, he holds me, and for the first time, I feel heard. I feel safe. He holds me tight and kisses the top of my head.

"I won't let anyone hurt you like that ever again, ok?" His voice is deep, and I nod my head against his chest. A man I've known for only a few weeks wants to protect me more than my own mother. I haven't felt this safe since my dad passed away, and I almost don't want to leave the side of the road. He lets me cry until I feel my breathing start to calm down, the anxiety blanketed by the warmth of his embrace. Then, when I pull away slowly, he looks me in the eyes.

"You're ok." It is more of a statement than a question, and I nod my head. I watch as his eyes go from soft and tender to something else. His jaw ticks, and he places a kiss on my forehead.

"Let's go get Alex." He ushers me back into the car, and I can tell he is upset. He gets into the car, and his hand finds its place in mine again.

"I just hope he isn't there so we can get Alex's things and leave," I say as he pulls the car back onto the road.

"Oh, I hope he is." He says as a sinister smile crosses his face for only a moment, then returns to furrowed brows and a ticking jaw. I haven't seen Jasper angry, but his anger fills the car, and for a second, I'm scared of what will happen if Craig is in that house.

When I start to recognize the town I left behind weeks ago, I pull out my phone to call Alex. He is waiting at his friend's house, so we head that way. My body is all nerves as we pull in front of the house, and I see Alex start to cross the yard. I can't stop my body from running out of the car to pull him into a hug.

"Oh, my God! I've missed you. Are you ok?" I hug him before pulling back to look at him. When I see his swollen split lip, my body feels like it wants to explode.

"Don't freak out. I'm ok. He just backhanded me. It looks a lot worse than it feels, ok?" He assures me, but I want to burn the world down at that very moment.

"Look, we can buy you new things; let's just get the fuck out of here and never look back," I tell him, not wanting to return to that house.

"I can't, Dani; I have to go back. I'll run in quick." He tries to convince me, but I don't want to hear any of it.

"Alex, we can get you more things. Nothing is worth going back into that house." I pull him to the car.

"Dad's things; I need to run in and at least get that. Please." He says, letting go of my hand. I know exactly what he's talking about. He has a box of Dad's things, an old pocket knife, and stuff like that.

"Fine, but I'm coming in with you. Let's go." My voice sounds shaky no matter how much I try to hide it.

When Alex gets into the car, I introduce him to Jasper. I can see Jasper take in the sight of his busted lip, and I know that if Craig is in that house, this won't be as easy as Alex thinks. I crack my knuckles as we pull up to our old house, not out of anger but out of nerves. I recognize the beat-up truck in the driveway and know Craig is in that house. I still can't believe she let him come back.

"We will be right back, ok. I promise." I tell Jasper, but he shakes his head and is already leaving the car. He doesn't wait for us as he walks up to the front door. He also doesn't knock as he walks into the house and holds the door open for us as we rush in behind him.

Thankfully, I can hear mom and Craig in the bedroom as I stand in the living room. The house looks even more disgusting than before I left. Alex takes off to his room, and I follow him to help him pack. When I walk into his room, I can tell he is trying to be quick and quiet.

"Who is that guy? Is he in the mafia or something?" Alex asks as he packs some clothes. I laugh because I know he thinks that because of how he dresses.

"I don't think so. He's my boss." I say as I pack in as much as I can grab. Alex grabs that box of dad's things from the top of his closet and puts it in his duffle bag. We both stop instantly when we hear the door down the hall open.

"Who the fuck are you?" I recognize Craig's voice, and Alex and I take off running out of the bedroom. When Craig sees us coming down the hall, he smiles.

"Oh, you think you going somewhere, boy?" He tries to walk towards us, but Jasper stands in the way.

"You guys go get in the car," Jasper says, and I didn't think his voice could sound any deeper. We move behind him to leave when I hear my mom.

"Dani? What are you doing here?" She calls out to me. I feel my skin flush with heat because I don't want to look at her. She looks horrible.

"I'm taking Alex, and we are leaving," I tell her as I walk with Alex to the front door.

"Oh really? You think you can just come here and call the shots in my fucking house? And who is this?" She slurs her words, obviously drunk.

"Look, I just want to take Alex and leave. This is my boss; He gave me a ride. We aren't here for any trouble; we just came here to get Alex's things. So we are leaving now." I won't give her what she wants; she won't get to me.

"So, you're fucking your boss? Wow, I bet daddy is really proud of his little raven." She laughs, and my anger starts to boil over. Hearing the nickname my dad gave me come out of her sloppy mouth makes me see red. How can she even speak about my dad after everything she's done?

"Yeah, and I wonder what he would think of you?" I say the words because I know they will hurt. Her laughter stops like she's been hit with his memory, and I enjoy putting her in her place.

"Get the fuck out of my house. Both of you, and don't come back." She turns away and returns to her room, where I'm sure she will finish off another bottle to drown the memory I've brought up. I don't let the tears betray me as I turn back to Alex, and we start to leave. I can feel Jasper start to follow behind us, and I'm grateful to get out of this house.

"Daddy Craig will let you come back anytime you want, Dani, Don't forget that." He calls out to me, and I hear the crash before we can make it out the door. Alex and I stand in the doorway and watch as Jasper has Craig up against the wall. Picture frames fall as Craig fights to get out of the hold Jasper has on him.

"You ever come near them again, and I will rip your fucking dick off and feed it to you. Do you understand, you worthless piece of shit!" Jasper roars in his face and then lets him go. Craig fixes his clothes and nods, embarrassed.

"Get the fuck…" Before Jasper takes two steps, he turns around and cuts Craig's words short with a punch dropping Craig on his ass. I cringe at the cracking sound heard across the room. Jasper doesn't stop there; he continues to rain punch after punch on top of him. I don't even realize my mom is standing there screaming for them to stop. I watch for a moment as Craig's body moves with each punch Jasper delivers. Finally, I run to Jasper and stop him mid-swing.

"Enough, Enough. Let's go, please. Jasper, Please." I tell him, and he comes out of whatever trance he is in. Standing up, he rolls up his sleeves and adjusts his clothes. I risk a glance at Craig as he turns to his side to spit up blood. My mom rushes to his side. "Get the fuck out of here, or I'm calling the cops!" she yells at us, helping Craig sit up.

Jasper returns to his calm demeanor as he follows me out the door. Alex comes to my side of the car and leans into me, "I think he is in the mafia." He says before getting into the back seat.

The car is silent for a few minutes until Jasper is the first to break the silence, "I'm sorry about that, Alex; you didn't need to see all of that." He says, gripping the steering wheel a little tighter. I can tell he feels bad for losing his cool.

"No way, man, that was badass. He had it coming for a long time. Thank you." Alex says, and this time I'm the one who reaches over to grab his hand. He glances toward me, and the corner of his mouth tips up into a small smile. I'm grateful for everything he has done tonight. But more importantly, I'm terrified because this man just finished breaking down every wall I've had, and now I sit here, open and vulnerable. I'm surprised as a smile crosses my face because even though I'm scared of these feelings for him, I still feel safe for the first time in a long time.

Chapter Ten

Jasper

I can't believe I did that; I lost control. I haven't lost control like that in years. I could have killed that man; the scary part is that I wouldn't have felt an ounce of regret. I couldn't leave that house with him thinking he got away with touching or talking to her that way. I got in the car, and I felt like I fucked up whatever it was we had going on. The start of something great could have ended in me losing control, but instead, she grabbed my hand. She holds my hand, and everything feels right again. How did we get to this point so quickly? She has hypnotized me from day one, but now it's different. Maybe it's the adrenaline still thrumming through my veins, but I want nothing more than to pull over and take her right here in this back seat, to tell her she's mine and no one will ever lay a fucking finger on her again.

Thankfully, her brother is in the backseat keeping me from coming on a little too strong. I am amazed by the strength of this woman now that I know where she has come from and what she has been through. I can't imagine living the life she has lived, losing her father, and having her life spiral so out of control. I would have lost my mind so long ago, but here she is, starting a new life for herself and her brother. Her strength is enough to make me worship her. Looking in the rearview mirror, I see her brother sleeping, and seeing his busted lip makes me cringe. I don't know what kind of kid he is or if he's a troublemaker, but he seems like a good kid. Either way, no kid, no person deserves to be backhanded.

"Thank you for tonight. I'm sorry for everything that happened." She says, breaking the silence. She looks back at Alex and smiles when she sees he has fallen asleep.

"Don't be sorry. I'm glad I came; I don't even want to think about what would have happened if I wasn't there." The thought brings back that burning in my chest. I know he would have hurt her if I hadn't been there to stop him.

"I'm just happy to have Alex out of there finally. I feel like I can relax now. He thinks you're in the mafia," She says with a small laugh.

"The mafia? Why?" I laugh. The last thing I need is for her brother to think I'm dangerous. Dani lives for this kid; I have nothing if I don't have his approval.

"I don't know because you dress like you stepped out of an episode of Peaky Blinders, and you're a total badass. You didn't even knock; you walked right in and handled business." She says with a nudge and a smile.

"What is Peaky Blinders? Are they in the mafia?" I ask, and her eyes go wide with shock.

"You've never seen Peaky Blinders? OK, we have to change that. You would love it. They aren't the mafia, but still, kind of, I guess." She says.

"Well, I assume they are very well-dressed, handsome individuals then." I tease.

"Maybe." She says, smiling and rolling her eyes.

"They are very handsome, and you should totally come over for a marathon night." Alex's voice says from the backseat, making us both laugh. Apparently, he wasn't really asleep, and I have enough of his approval for an invitation.

"I'll have to do that. How are you feeling back there?" I ask. He smiles, still staring out the window.

"I'm good, but I could use a bathroom now." He says, leaning forward.

We pull over at the nearest gas station since I need to fill up for the ride home anyways. Alex comes out of the store with two bags full of chips and candy while sipping on a big gulp. Dani follows behind, rolling her eyes and laughing, carrying two cups of coffee. She hands me the cup, and we make the long trip back home. She is a different person with Alex; she seems softer and happier.

When we finally pull into her driveway, she wakes up Alex and runs inside with him while I wait in the car. Now that I've seen where she comes from, I can tell why she felt so guilty being here. Our town is quiet, sometimes too quiet. People are not hanging out in the street, making it hard to even pass down the road. The yards are cleaner. I hate that some towns are forgotten and left to fall deeper into despair. The whole experience tonight makes me appreciate our little town so much more.

Dani gets back in the car, and we head back to my place. As tired as I am, I don't want the night to end, but I know she needs to pick up her car and head back home. Pulling into the driveway, I put the car in park, but we both don't move.

"I know I've said it already, but thank you. I know tonight has been crazy, and I understand if you want to go back to the way things were before. I have a ton of baggage, and there is still the fact that you're my boss and..." She tries to ramble on, but I lean over the console and kiss her. She kisses me back, and I would ask her to come upstairs if I was a selfish man.

"Take the next few days off to get Alex settled in. Take as long as you need. But understand me when I say there is no way we could go back to the way things were before because I have been under your spell since the day I met you in your driveway." Tucking her hair behind her ear, she kisses me again.

"You must be insane to want anything to do with me after tonight." She says, shaking her head like she can't believe what I'm saying.

"I was never really insane, except upon occasions...." I start the quote, and she smiles.

"When my heart was touched." She finished the quote and kissed me again, making me dizzy with lust—a woman who can easily quote Poe and has a kiss that intoxicates you. If I don't get her out of this car soon and on her way home, I may throw her over my shoulder and carry her inside myself.

"Goodnight, Dani," I say though my body is screaming hateful words at me.

"Goodnight, Jasper." She says before she gets out of the car and waves goodbye while I gather myself until she backs out the driveway. The exhaustion finally hits after pulling out my keys to unlock the door. This can go down in history as the longest night of my life. Turning the key in the lock, I hear music playing from inside the house. I turn the handle, but my key won't unlock the door.

"What the fuck?" I pull the key out to check it and try again. I know I'm not that exhausted that I don't recognize my own house key. Where is that music coming from? I walk across the porch and look through the window that leads to the office, the music is coming from the office, and it is loud.

I don't know if it's cloudy or bright.....

The words send a chill all over my body as I back away from the window. That song, it's her song. Memories of that night flash across my mind like bolts of lightning.

I only have eyes for you.....

What is going on? I need to get into the house now. I pull out my keys again to try one more time as the music seems to get louder. My hands feel clammy, and I drop the keys. My chest tightens; she can't be here.

"Fuck!" I grab the keys and try to unlock the door. As the lock clicks, I swing open the door, and it's silent in the house. The music isn't playing anymore. I rush into the office expecting to see someone, but the office is empty. I checked the record player to see that there was no record on it, and it's still unplugged from the other day. Something isn't right here; am I losing my mind? Stepping slowly out into the foyer, I stop to listen for any sound that might explain what's happening. I'm left with nothing but silence. It's been a long day, and I'm exhausted, so I double-check the locks and walk through each room downstairs just to make sure no one is here. She can't be here.

The house is empty, and I am losing my mind. I head upstairs, briefly turning back to check for any signs of movement. My body shakes with a chill as I turn my back to the stairs and walk to my bedroom. The room is dark and welcoming, although I'm still confused. I know I'm exhausted, but nothing can explain what just happened. I lock my bedroom door before walking to the middle of the room and throwing myself across the bed. I don't even feel myself falling asleep.

My alarm goes off for the third time, the sounds blaring through the still quiet house. I must have passed out when my body finally hit the bed. I'm still in the clothes from last night, and I'm grateful I gave Dani the day off because I'm a mess. I take a shower and work up the effort to go downstairs and start the day. As I finally make it downstairs, the stairs creak, and I stop in the foyer to look around. Flashbacks of last night have me waiting for someone to walk out of some dark corner or for the music to start blaring again. I shake off the thoughts running through my head because I can't begin to get spooked by things like this in my line of work. Everything has an explanation, and I'm sure it was nothing. I recognize that I'm lying to myself, but at this point, I have no other choice.

The day goes a bit slower and a lot quieter without Dani here. I don't regret giving her the day off, but I realize I miss her. I had food delivered to them around lunchtime because, apparently, that is my love language. I want to make sure she doesn't have to worry about anything so she can rest up and come back to work. I don't know how I did this all on my own before her—being alone with the bodies, the quiet, lonely nights. I lose track of time working on a body and realize it is getting late. I decide to call it a night and return the body to cold storage when I hear a noise come from upstairs. I stop immediately and listen. When I hear footsteps from upstairs, my pulse quickens, and I move quickly to the stairs but remain quiet. As I climb the stairs, the door opens, and my legs almost give out.

I exhale, the adrenaline pumping through my body when I see Dani standing at the top of the stairs.

"Working late?" She asks.

"You scared the shit out of me," I say with a nervous laugh as I finish making my way up to greet her. Wrapping my arms around her, I feel the tension in my body release.

"I didn't mean to scare you. I just wanted to stop by and thank you for lunch. You didn't have to do that, but it was delicious. Alex is in a food coma as we speak." She says.

"It's OK. Some weird things have been happening around here lately, and I let myself get spooked. I'm glad you enjoyed the food. How's Alex?" I ask, still trying to slow my heart rate so I can mentally function.

"You sure you're OK?" She asks, looking at me concerned.

"Yeah, I'm fine," I reassure her; knowing it was her footsteps, and not someone else is enough to bring me back to sanity, or at least the last shred of sanity I'm hanging on to.

"OK, Well, he's doing good. I plan on taking him around town this weekend. I think he's going to love it here. But what do you mean weird stuff has been happening?" She says, following me. She stops at the base of the stairs, and I sense her hesitation about coming upstairs.

"It's nothing, just random things that I feel silly for even mentioning now. You coming upstairs?" I ask, hoping that she will say yes. I don't bother to explain further about what's been happening because I can barely make sense of it in my head, let alone out loud. A moment passes when I think she will say no, but then she nods and follows me up the stairs. It has been years since anyone has been up here; I keep work and my living areas completely separate. Having her up here is like inviting her to my house; it feels intimate. When you come up the stairs, it opens into a living area with a bathroom and two bedrooms down the hallway. I watch as she looks around, taking everything in.

"So, I finally get to see what's up here. I must say I'm impressed." She says as we both sit on the sofa. I know why she's impressed because the living space up here is surrounded by overflowing bookshelves, with the exception of a tiny mini bar. I could call it a mini bar, but it's just a bourbon decanter and a few glasses. I've always liked to have a glass of bourbon after a long day, and paired with a good book is nothing short of perfection.

"Well, thank you. I knew I would get you up here someday." I tease.

"Oh really?" Her eyes lock with mine, and it feels like the air has been sucked from the room. She always has this effect on me; sometimes, I fear that her eyes can see through me.

"No, not really. I'm glad you're here, though. I missed having you here today." I say, resting my hand on hers. She scoots closer to me, and I can't hide its effect on my body. The sexual tension has been heavy in the air the last few times we have been together, and I'm trying desperately to be a gentleman as my heart rate picks right back up. I don't want her to think I brought her up her expecting anything. I just didn't want her to leave yet. Regardless of me trying not to make my feelings obvious, I can tell she also feels the tension. Even in the dim lighting, I can see her cheeks flush. Leaning closer to me, she kisses my lips softly, and that's when I feel it. Her hand slowly runs up my thigh, and my skin feels hot.

"How about you show me just how much you missed me?" She whispers against my lips, and I'm unhinged.

Chapter Eleven

Dani

I can feel his length pressed against me as I straddle his lap. I won't lie and say I didn't have this planned out in my head before coming here. I won't deny myself happiness any longer. This man is my idea of perfection, almost like he was made just for me. I don't care if he's my boss, I don't care about the age difference, none of that matters. He is kind, sexy, and smart, and I won't let my past or anything hold me back any longer. The tension leading up to this moment has been driving me insane. So for my sanity's sake, I will be reckless tonight.

The way he is kissing me makes the world tilt, and it is far more than a kiss; his touch radiates down my body, traveling heat down my spine as he takes from me. He takes over my body with his desire as his tongue slides past my parted lips. The steady beat of my heart moves down my body to the apex of my thighs. I am a mindless slave to his touch, and I want his lips and hands on every part of me. Threading my hands through his hair, I tug it, moving his lips to my neck. He lets out a slight hiss and follows the curve of my neck with his kisses. When he grips my ass roughly and lifts me off the sofa with him, I let out a moan that sounds more like a growl. He carries me across the room towards the bedrooms, never taking his lips off of me.

I laugh when he kicks open the door to his bedroom, and he lets out a breathy laugh against the sensitive skin of my neck. Throwing me on the bed with a bounce, I prop myself up to take in the sight of this man before me. I watch as he pulls off his shirt and shows me the body he has been hiding under those suits. The room is dark, but the moon shines perfectly on his body from the window. As he unbuckles his belt, his dark eyes never leave mine. His pants fall to the floor, and he stands before me in just his tight boxers letting my eyes feast on the sight of his toned body. He has that muscular V shape that leads straight to the bulging imprint of his cock. It isn't until I see him smile that I notice my jaw hanging. That toned body isn't the only thing he has been hiding under that suit because I'm staring at something that I'm sure will destroy me in all the best ways.

"Come here." I don't recognize my own voice as he comes closer to crawl into the bed, but I stop him before he can crawl into bed with me.

"Stand right here." I motion to the side of the bed instead, and he listens. As he stands there, I let him watch me as I undress. I almost giggle when I see his dick twitch begging to be released. The cool air greets my exposed skin, and I crawl over to him. On my knees, I pull him closer and trail my kisses down his body, tasting every part of him. The rich woodsy smell of his cologne mixes with the faint smell of the chemicals we work with, and now it's my favorite smell; cologne and formaldehyde, his own signature scent. When I get to the waste band of his boxers, I pull them down, releasing his cock with a bounce. Instead of immediately taking him into my mouth, I lay down on my back, wrap my arms around his knees, and pull him closer. His body jolts when I suck each of his balls tenderly into my mouth.

"Fuck, Dani." He breathes out, surprised by what I'm doing to him. A sense of pride mingles with my arousal at the fact that I took him by surprise. I trail my own hands down my body that I have on display for him. I pinch my hardened nipples as I lick the length of the bottom of his cock. "You are so fucking beautiful," he breathes the words out as I continue to suck and lick at his balls.

"I want you to fuck my face," I say before I take his length into my mouth. I smile around his cock as he is forced to lean forward and brace himself. I start to feel him thrust slowly into my mouth at first. I can tell he is holding back, so I reach around and pull him deeper into my mouth. My lips feel tight around his girth, and when I gag around his cock something unleashes in him. I can tell he likes the sound of me gagging, so I continue to do it, and his pace picks up as he thrusts into my mouth faster. I trail my hand down my body and start to circle my clit with my fingers as I listen to his moans. He grabs my breast and pinches my nipple enough to make me moan around his cock, and I taste the sweet pre-cum he releases.

Thrusting deep into my throat, he pulls out and steps back. "You've had enough. On your knees." His voice is husky but stern. I get up onto my knees in the bed, slightly dizzy from the lack of oxygen and the upside position I was in. Closing the small space between us, he threads his hand in my hair, pulling back to expose my neck. His mouth sucks and nips at my neck while I feel the hand that was in my hair trail down my body slowly, leaving chills as it moves to my pussy. When he slides his fingers into me, I gasp at the relief it gives me.

"You're so fucking wet for me, Dani.Fuck." He moans in my ear as he pushes his fingers into me and circles my clit with his thumb. My body almost melts into his as he applies just the right amount of pressure like he knows exactly what he's doing. I feel my hips jerk as I ride his fingers, aching for release.

"Don't you dare cum yet." He says, gripping my jaw and forcing me to stare into his eyes. He doesn't stop fingering me, and I feel my release is getting close. "Come on, get close. There you go. You want to cum for me?" He asks, and I nod my head in his hand. I can't control my breathing as I start to feel myself coming undone, and that's when he pulls his fingers out of me, denying me my release. Holding up his fingers, showing me my arousal, he sucks them into his mouth.

I stare as he closes his eyes and hums with pleasure at the taste of me on his fingers. "The first time I make you cum will be with me between your thighs; I want to taste every bit of it. Lay down," he demands. Our eyes are sealed to each other as I lay down; I have never had a man look at me the way he is looking at me now. I feel his eyes take in every inch of my bare skin as if they are physically caressing each dip and curve. This man will devour me, mind, body, and soul.

Chapter Twelve

Jasper

I almost came in her mouth when she told me to fuck her face. I didn't expect her to be so dominant in the bedroom, so I had to fight to control myself. She has a way of being assertive but still gives me the control I like and listens to my commands. I watch her with a hunger I haven't felt in years as she lies in bed waiting for me. I crawl into bed, and her eyes never leave mine, still heavy and filled with lust. I can't wait to hear what she sounds like when she comes undone.

Positioning myself between her legs, I move my hand slowly up the smooth, creamy skin of her inner thigh until I'm sliding my two fingers over her cunt. I can't stop myself from spreading her open wide; seeing her arousal glisten sends electricity to my cock. I take in the sight of her bare to me. The female body is a work of art, and Dani is a fucking masterpiece. The sound of her soft whimper almost sends me over the edge. I push my fingers in, and my two fingers are wrapped in the warmth of her pussy again. My head tilts back as I exhale my frustration that it is only my fingers experiencing her sweet warmth. I move them in and out, slightly curling my fingers like I'm beckoning her arousal to come closer. She sucks in a deep breath through her nose as I continue working my fingers, exploring her every whimper, mesmerized by how her hips jerk and move at my touch as I bring her close to the edge again. I place a soft kiss on her stomach as I pull my fingers out. She wants her release, her eyes hooded and pinned on me, and I've denied her twice.

My lips trail kisses down her thighs, her calves, and across her ankle as I take her foot in my hands. I press my thumbs into the arch of her foot, massaging before I softly kiss the side. She groans in pleasure. Then she gasps as I take her toe into my mouth, sucking softly. Her eyes widen as her breathing gets faster. I take her toe into my mouth again, trailing my tongue across the soft skin, watching her nipples peak as she closes her eyes while sucking in that bottom lip. Putting her foot down beside me, I stare at her body once more. The gentle curves of her breast, her wide hips, forming lines the greatest of artists couldn't replicate. I make my way back up her thigh with wet kisses until I get so close to where she wants me her legs shake and her hips thrust up, begging to meet my tongue.

"Please, Please, Please." She begs, and it's like music to my ears. I position myself and stare up at her before I dip my tongue in her arousal and lick up to her clit. Her body jolts and gyrates as I pull back slightly. Then before she can whimper again, I dive back into her sex, sucking her clit into my mouth and flattening my tongue against it. I roll my tongue against her sensitive bud as I suck gently, and she rides my face. I feel her hands in my hair, and I know if I try to pull away again, she won't let me. She is prepared to smother me in her pussy, and I can't think of a better way to go. She tastes so damn good, and I fist my cock to relieve the pressure. I feel her body start to shake, and I know her orgasm is coming, so I dip my two fingers into her, and that's when she comes undone. Unintelligible noises come from her mouth as she rides the wave of euphoria on my face and fingers. I smile at how beautiful she sounds as she cries out.

"That's a good girl. Look at you; you ready for more?" I praise her as I crawl up her body and suck her nipple into my mouth.

"Fuck yes," she breathes out, and I smile against her soft skin.

Once I move forward, there is no going back; I will be under her spell, addicted to her touch. I'm already missing the taste of her on my tongue. Sitting up between her legs, I fist my cock, and at that moment, her eyes gaze down at my hands, then the corner of her mouth perks up slightly, giving me the devil's grin. And just like that, I am lost. I smile back at her as I grip her thighs roughly and pull her into me. As I push inside of her, our bodies fuse together. I move my cock slowly at first, letting her adjust to my size. Moving in and out, I can see my cock covered in her wetness, and I pick up the pace. The sound of our heavy breathing fills the room while we lose ourselves in the moment. I shove my hips forward, making her breast move enticingly with each thrust. Her black nails dig into my sheets as I start to feel her clench onto my cock, sucking me in as if I belong there.

"That's it, baby, cum for me; I want to hear you. I want you to wake the fucking dead with your screams, cum!" I say with each thrust as she reaches her orgasm, and I feel her pulse around my cock. Watching the way her stomach caves in as she takes a deep breath, her prominent ribs have me wanting to place a kiss on each one, appreciating her anatomy with every inch of creamy skin, every bone in her body.

"You're so beautiful when you cum, baby," I say, slowing my pace as she finishes riding out her orgasm.

"But I want one more," I say, and her eyes widen as I pick up my pace and start to circle her clit with my fingers. It doesn't take long before she is cumming around my cock again, and I can't stand it any longer.

"You ready to take my cum?" I pant as I thrust faster, prepared to pull out.

"I want your cum deep inside me." She moans, and I almost lose it. She notices my expression.

"I have an IUD; now cum inside me, Jasper. Now. Fill me up." She moves her hips to match my thrusts, and that's all it takes. My balls tighten as I hold my breath and come with a full-body sensation that has me dizzy. I feel my cock pulsing while buried deep inside of her. The room spins, and I feel almost light-headed, intoxicated with the release.

Before I pull out, I lean into her and kiss her deeply.

"You're fucking amazing. You know that?" I ask her, and she smiles against my lips.

"You're not too bad yourself." She teases, and I let out a breathy laugh. We don't get dressed right away; we just both lay there, almost stunned by what just happened. If I thought there was no going back before, now it's truly impossible. I have never been with a woman like Dani, dominant yet passive.

Bang Bang

The sound makes us both sit upright in bed and stare at each other, straining our senses to see if we can hear it again and where it's coming from.

Bang Bang Bang

I bolt out of bed and start to get dressed. If that is someone at the door again, I will lose it. Dani follows my lead and starts getting dressed as well before standing close behind me.

"Jasper, is that the front door?" She whispers behind me as we make our way out of the room and down the stairs. My eyes are burning holes into that front door, waiting to hear the knock again.

Bang Bang Bang

We both jump in the direction of the sound and when we realize where it's coming from, a chill runs down my spine. I can see the fear on her face and know she knows where the sound is coming from.

"Get behind me," I say to her, even though she is already in position and waiting for me to lead the way. The sound isn't coming from the front door; the sound is coming from the basement. The quiet basement where nothing could possibly be making noise. As I open the door, a cold gust of wind envelops me, and I get the chills again. My eyes frantically check every corner of the rooms as we walk through.

Bang Bang

"Shit," Dani yelps behind me making me jump. What the fuck is going on here. I know the bodies I have down here are definitely dead, so unless we have somehow transported into an episode of The Walking Dead, there shouldn't be a fucking sound down here. I know where the sound is coming from, and my body dreads every slow, silent step toward the cold storage room. I close my eyes, saying a silent prayer as Dani grips my arm behind me before I push open the door.

The room is empty and cold, and nothing seems out of place until I notice where the sound had to have been coming from. Earlier, when Dani scared the shit out of me, I must have left the door to one of the bodies open. I take another look around the room, expecting to see the body that was supposed to be in there to come running out of the dark corner of the room. Instead, I pull out the body I was working on earlier and confirm that it is, in fact, still dead. Looking at Dani's terrified face, I start to laugh. She joins me in the hilarity of the situation.

"I guess you really did wake the dead with your screams," I tease. After the relief of knowing we don't have a corpse walking around, we both start to think about the situation. I can tell she is trying to figure out the noise, just like I am.

"How was it making all that noise, though? It's not like there is a draft in here to make it bang closed like that." She pointed out what we both were thinking but didn't want to say out loud.

"I don't want to scare you, but this isn't the first weird thing that has happened in the past few days. I think we may have a ghost." I put humor behind my words, but I won't lie and say I don't believe it. I have had some unexplainable things happen, and ghosts are the most logical explanation.

"You believe in ghosts?" She teases.

"Honestly, I'm not sure," I say, wishing I could be someone who doesn't believe that what's been happening is possibly a restless spirit. I try not to let my expression show my thoughts as the memories flood my brain.

"Well, I do believe in ghosts, so I'm getting my ass out of here. I should probably head back home anyway." She says, pulling herself into my arms. She looks up at me and kisses me softly. The last thing on my mind is ghosts; I can get lost with her.

"Maybe they want a show, round two?" I laugh, and she rolls her eyes with a smile.

"Sounds fun, but I'll be back on Monday. Don't forget you have that conference thing this weekend. I put the directions in your bag." She says in that tone that if I push a little harder, she may just give in. I let her lead the way upstairs, and we say our goodbyes. When she leaves, the house feels empty again, but my chest is so full of warmth that I barely notice. She's perfection, and I am counting the days until Monday.

Chapter Thirteen

Dani

"So, you came home late last night." Alex throws himself on the couch beside me and looks at me with a smirk. I was lost in thoughts of last night that I didn't even hear him come into the room. The mug in my hand is no longer steaming. I take a sip to gather my thoughts on what I will say.

"Yeah, I just had a few things to take care of at work," I explain, but I can tell he isn't buying it.

"Oh, I'm sure you took care of things." He teases and laughs. I punch him in the shoulder without even spilling a drop of my coffee.

"Ouch, what the hell, I'm joking. I like the guy. I mean, he is your boss, though. Isn't that a little weird?" He asks.

"Surprisingly, no, not really. I met him the first day I got here and had no clue he was my boss. So we were both surprised. He's a nice guy, though." I say, remembering that day in the bookstore. I have since finished that book, and he was right; I did love it.

"Well, you're happy, I can tell. You don't have that giant stick sticking out of your ass, and you actually smile a little." He teases me again, and I give him another punch.

"Geez, have you also been lifting weights since you been here? Gosh, I approve, ok? I like him. That's what I'm trying to say. He seems like one of the good guys." He says, nudging my knee.

The knock on the door surprises me since it's Saturday, and I know Jasper has that conference thing today. I can hardly contain my excitement when I open the door and see Mrs. Janet's smiling face. What is happening to me? Alex is right; I've become a happy version of my previous self. The fact that smiling doesn't feel weird anymore must mean something.

"Danielle, my girl! I'm sorry it's taken me so long to visit. How are you?" She grabs me into a hug. I hear Alex come into the foyer, and she lets me go to rush up to him like she has known us both for years.

"You must be Alex. Look at how handsome you are; you will fit in just fine here. I'm sure of it. Have you met the Fenning boys yet? They are your age and really good boys. I think you would all get along just fine." She rambles on without letting us get a word in.

"I have some coffee made if you want some." I offer; she agrees and enters the kitchen after pinching Alex's cheek. I laugh at how shocked he is by her friendliness. She can be a little much at first, but she probably has the biggest heart out of anyone I have ever known. We both sit at the table with our mugs and catch up. I fill her in on why Alex is here already, and I think it's the first time I've ever seen her frown.

"I'm just happy you got him out of there, and you are both here and safe now. My heart breaks for you, Danielle, that you had to go through that." She takes my hand in hers, and it's a gesture I'm not used to, but I welcome it.

"Well, I had help getting him out of there. Jasper came along, and I think it wouldn't have been so easy if it weren't for him." I say and watch as her face changes again.

"Jasper Cooley drove you hours away to get your brother? What a nice man." She says with a knowing smirk. I can tell she is fishing for information. I smile at her attempt.

"He is a very nice man. A brilliant and handsome man." I say with a smile, and she squeals like a young girl.

"Oh my goodness. I couldn't imagine a more perfect pair. He is a very handsome man. I must say he is a kind heart and deserves happiness. You both do." she says.

"You don't think it's weird? I mean, he's my boss," I ask. She scoffs at me with a slap on the hand.

"As if. Life is short, my love. Everything will work out as it should, and you both have been through so much; you both deserve this. Have fun with it. See where it goes." She smiles, and I can tell in the silent moment that passes she is thinking of her husband. She's right, life is short, and I have wasted so much of it worrying about things that I shouldn't have. Alex joins us at the table, and we finish catching up before she heads out.

"She's like one of those grandmas from the movies. I guarantee she can make an amazing batch of cookies." Alex laughs, still shocked at how Mrs. Janet's personality can fill a room.

"She's special. I swear, she broke down every wall I tried to keep up. She just has a way of making you feel good. I adore her." I say as I rinse out our mugs. When I turn around, Alex is smiling.

"What?" I ask.

"Nothing, I just feel different here. You are different here. I feel like this is how it all should have been. If dad hadn't died, this is what life could have been. How is it possible to feel happy and angry at the same time?" He asks

"I'm not sure yet. But, I will say the anger starts to fade a little more each day," I say as he nods and looks out the window. I know the anger he has for what we have been through will take time to go away. I have to remind myself daily that we are here and safe now.

"Hey, how about we get out and explore the town? I have to get some groceries anyway, so you can pick out a few of your favorite things." I offer, and he's out of the chair and putting on shoes before I can even finish getting dressed.

I bring him to all my favorite spots, and we explore new ones together. I think this is the happiest I've been in a long time. I look at Alex and know he feels the same; this is what peace feels like. A sense of pride swells in my chest, knowing I was able to pull us out of there. I don't even wonder if our mom misses us because I know she's not. She has her drugs and boyfriend and no longer has to deal with us. So I guess we both got our own versions of paradise in the end.

After exploring, we finish the day at the grocery store, where Alex fills the buggy with pizza, pizza rolls, hot Cheetos, regular Cheetos, and zebra cakes. I stare at the cart, and he gives me an exhausted look.

"Come on; I'm a growing boy. This is what my body needs to be strong and disgusting." He laughs. I don't argue because I live off of coffee and pasta when I remember to eat. I am in no position to debate with anyone over their eating habits. When we get back home, Alex cooks a pizza for us both and grabs a zebra cake before making his way up to his bedroom. He will spend the rest of the night playing his game while I curl up with my book.

This is what life is now, and I take a moment to be grateful. Things can be easy, which is still an unfamiliar feeling. How is that when you are so accustomed to the chaos that when there is none, you feel lost? I feel like I'm waiting for something to happen that will turn my world upside down again, like this sense of peace is a cruel joke. There were times when I thought I must have done something terrible in a past life to deserve the cards I was dealt in this one.

Before I can sit down, I hear my phone ring and smile when I see who it is.

"Miss me already?" I answer.

"You have no idea. But unfortunately, that's not the only reason I'm calling. I just got a callout, and I'm still about two hours out. So I just need you to be there to receive the body. You don't have to do the workup. I can do it when I get home." He says.

"No, it's fine. I can get it done. I'll handle it." I say.

"I don't know how I managed before you. You spoil me; you know that." He says.

"Oh, do I? Well, I might take my time so that I can be there when you get back. Then I can really spoil you." I tease.

"Did I say I was two hours out? I meant one." He laughs.

"Don't rush; I'll wait for you. Be careful driving back." I say before we hang up, and I let Alex know I will be heading over to work. He gives me a knowing smile, and all I can do is roll my eyes. Before I grab my keys, I stop to look in the mirror, and the smile still hasn't left my face since I hung up the phone. The expression still looks weird on me, but I'm getting used to it.

When I get to the mortuary, the van is waiting. I let them in and printed the reports, starting on the body. I don't mind being alone; not having Jasper here allows me to work faster. He is a nice distraction, and I try not to show it. He is confident enough; he doesn't need me hiking up his ego. I laugh to myself because a month ago, I thought that the men here would be like the guy at the convenience store. I was set on the fact that romance would not be a distraction for me, and here I am, falling for my boss. I shake my head at the thought of how quickly I let myself fall into his arms. I have never moved so quickly with a man, and I start to feel a sense of doubt before I hurry and push it away. I need to start taking risks and not being scared of being happy. Why is it so hard to believe that this may be a good thing?

Sure, he has this dark and mysterious thing going for him, but that's what I love about him. Maybe he is a little too mysterious because now that I think about it, I don't really know much about him. I see the surface things, his favorite books, and things like that, but I don't really know that much about him. That doubt starts to creep up again, and I make a mental note to talk to him about it. He knows so much about me and where I come from, but I don't know much about him.

I'm just about finished with the body when I hear the door to the basement open. The smile that crosses my face quickly fades when I hear a voice call out, "Hello?"

That's not the voice I was expecting. Making my way down the hall, I see a woman standing at the desk, she quickly turns to me, and I watch as her eyes look me up and down.

"Who are you? Where is Jasper?" She asks as she looks behind me. She is tall and beautiful in a strict sort of way. Her mouth pressed into a hard line as I walk behind the desk.

"I'm sorry he's not here, but he should be here soon. I'm Dani; I'm his assistant." I say, putting my hand out to shake hers.

She looks at my hand, and a look of concern crosses her eyes as she tucks her long blonde hair behind her ear. I pull my hand back slowly when she doesn't take it, and I feel my stomach start to roll. Who is she?

"His assistant? Yeah, right. Well, you can leave now." She says as I watch her eyes start to gloss over.

"I'm sorry. Who are you?" I try to take the defensiveness out of my voice, but who the hell does she think she is? She looks at me with wide eyes that I'm sure would strike me dead if she could.

"I'm his wife, and I said you can leave now." She stares me down as she delivers the punch of her words, and I feel my head dizzy for a moment.

"His wife? I'm sorry, I've worked here for over a month, and he never mentioned you. I apologize." I'm trying not to choke on my words as my happy little world comes crashing down before me.

"I'm sure he hasn't. He doesn't want you to know about me. I'm sure he doesn't want you to know about a lot of things. Now, I won't say it again. You can leave my house and don't worry about coming back. Don't worry about thanking me, either. Just get the fuck out." Her words drip with anger, and I can't do anything but walk out because I am in the wrong here. I don't say a word; I give her the same stare she gives me as I grab my things and walk out.

I don't let my tears fall into I'm in my car. Pulling out of the driveway, I don't go home; I park on the side of the road and let myself process what just fucking happened. I can't go home yet; I can't let Alex see me like this. What would he think of me messing with a married man? I had no idea, but I didn't even think to ask. I just assumed he was single. Thinking back to my conversation with Mrs. Janet, she didn't even mention her. Are they separated, and now she is coming back? I have no clue what to think, and that's because I know nothing about this fucking man. I am so fucking stupid. I punch the steering wheel because the alternative is driving back to wait for him to get there to explain.

If he was married, how could he do the things he did with me? Because men are fucking pigs Dani, that's why. I was so blinded by the thought that I could actually be happy and have it all. I was greedy, thinking I could have a new town, a new job, a new house, and a happy relationship. Life has never been that good to me, and I was stupid to think that would ever change. I should have known. I shake off the remaining tears and get myself together. I don't care about him or his wife; all I care about is that I just got my brother settled in here, and now I have to find a new job. We can't go back; I won't allow us to return to that place.

I have always done what needed to be done, no matter how hard it was. My only focus should have been on Alex and me, not Jasper. I wipe the remaining tears and put the car in drive. I will not let this break me; I have been through worse and will get through this. Fuck him and his wife; I am not a homewrecker; I did nothing wrong. The best thing to do, the right thing for me to do, is walk away. I can find another job, and I have enough in savings to help until then. I don't need Jasper or any man, for that matter. I let the anger take over because I can't take the feeling of my heart breaking as I pull into the driveway.

Chapter Fourteen

Jasper

As I get closer to the house, I have to push down the eager erection I have pushing at the steering wheel. I know Dani is home waiting for me, and it's such a good feeling. Although the feeling is good, it is still odd after years of being alone. I knew Dani coming into my life would help me with my problems, but I had no idea she would be this helpful. She has completely quieted my mind and taken over like some enchantress.

Pulling into the driveway, I look at the place momentarily before getting out. At one point, I thought I would lose all of this, but now I am with a thriving business and a gorgeous woman waiting for me inside. Smiling wide, I get out of the car and make my way to the front door. I notice the house is dark and quiet when I open the door. Closing the door behind me, I hear the faint sound of laughter coming from upstairs. I don't push down the erection this time as it strains against the seams of my pants. This wouldn't be the first time Dani surprised me, thinking back to that first night we were together. I quietly make it up the stairs and see the bedroom door closed. The light behind the door shuts off, and I know she's in there waiting for me. Arousal courses through my body as I picture her behind the door, naked and waiting for me. I can almost taste her on my tongue already. Pushing the door open, I look into the dark empty room. The laughter I heard earlier is nearly a whisper; it's so quiet, coming from the corner of the room.

"Dani," I call into the darkness, but she says nothing.

"Come here," I say as I start to unbuckle my belt. Still, she doesn't respond.

Finally, I make out her figure in the corner of the room, but she is looking away from me. I'm confused at what game she is trying to play, but I still play along.

"You trying to make me beg for it?" I say to her as I start to cross the room. My steps halt when I hear the soft whimper. Is she crying?

"Dani? You ok?" I don't wait for her to answer; instead, I turn on the lights. When I look back to the corner, I see it's empty. The figure I saw is gone, and the room is completely empty. I stand in the center of the room, trying to make sense of what happened. I clearly heard her and saw her right here. Walking out of the room, I reach the top of the stairs before calling out for her again.

"Dani, you here?" My voice echoes in the silent house. Pulling out my phone, I call Dani. I wait at the top of the stairs to hear her ringtone, giving away her hiding spot, but I don't hear anything. After a few rings, I'm sent to voicemail. I tried to call again, hoping she would answer, but still nothing. I cross the floor to the bedroom to check one more time when the text message comes in.

Dani: You can stop calling me. I'm fine. Just leave me alone.

What the fuck is going on? Rushing down the stairs, I go to the basement, thinking I might find her there, but as I make my way to the embalming room, I see the body still lying on the table. Everything looks complete, but she never picked up the body. I check cold storage only to find the room is empty as well. I feel a sick feeling in my stomach as I text her back.

Is everything ok? What's going on?

She starts to text back, but I watch her erase her response at least three times before the message comes through.

Dani: Why don't you ask your wife?

I have to read the words a few times because my brain can't comprehend what she's saying over the loud ringing in my ears. This can't be fucking happening. How could she possibly know about her? I hear the faint sound of laughter again, and my body goes cold. This can't be happening. I need to fix this. Dani is the only one keeping me together; I can't lose her. I have made too much progress since she has come into my life. I won't let this happen.

I go back upstairs, cursing the air, as I fall into my office chair. I call Dani again because I need to explain myself; I need to fix this. After a few rings, I finally hear her answer.

"Jasper, please just leave me alone." She answers in an angry hushed tone. Hearing a door close, I know she must be trying to escape, so Alex doesn't listen.

"Dani, I need to talk to you. I'm begging you for a chance to explain." I sound pathetic, but I don't care.

"Explain what! How your angry wife you never told me about fired me tonight!" Her words don't make sense.

"What do you mean she fired you?" I ask as my body chills over even more.

"Your wife confronted me tonight; yeah, she came in wondering who the fuck I was and why I was there. She told me to get the fuck out of her house and not to come back. How else could you possibly explain that, Jasper?" She sounds like she is on the verge of tears. I am stuck speechless. How is this possible?

"Hello?" she practically yells into the phone, pulling me from my thoughts.

"You saw my wife tonight? In-person? In the house?" I ask.

"Are you fucking stupid? Yes, Jasper, your wife. Look, leave me alone. I don't want your explanation; I don't want anything from you." I can tell she is about to hang up, and I panic.

"No, NO, no, wait, Dani. I have to explain this to you, but there is no way I could do it over the phone. I promise you; this is not what you think. Please let me come there to explain." I ask.

"Yeah, you must be stupid if you think I will let you come here and argue with me with Alex here. You got caught. Ok? Take your loss like a big boy and move the fuck on." The fiesty part of her I knew was lying low has come out, and her words catch me off guard.

"Come here then. Please. I swear on everything; you got this all wrong. Please, I am not a begging man, but I am begging now. If, after I explain, you still don't believe me, I'll leave you alone. I won't contact you at all. All I'm asking is for a chance to explain this." I wait for her answer while my heart pulses in my ears.

"Fuck, fine, Jasper." She says and hangs up before I can say another word.

The minutes seem like hours while I wait for her car to pull up. Finally, when the headlights light up the front window, I jump up, ready to explain the impossible. She doesn't even knock. She walks right in and stops in the foyer staring at me as I sit at the base of the stairs. Standing up, I start to walk over to her, and she crosses her arms telling me with her body to back the fuck off.

"Come upstairs, I will pour us a drink, and I can explain. We both seem very confused about what happened here tonight.?" I say as I put my hand out. She almost laughs at it.

"Yeah, right. We can go in the office." She walks past me and sits in the chair, showing me just how cold she can be. She is done with me, and nothing I say will change this. As I follow her into the office, I fight the urge to curse the air again.

"So, you are saying that my wife came into the house tonight and fired you," I ask again because I still can't understand it.

"I already explained this; I'm not about to waste my time." She says, rolling her eyes and standing up. I can't fight my body as I rush toward her trying to stop her.

"Don't fucking touch me, Jasper." She pushes me away, and I can feel my heart break. This shouldn't be happening.

"Dani, my wife is dead! Ok!" I yell over her, and she goes silent.

"Wow, that's your explanation." She looks at me like I'm the scum of the earth.

"Dani, it's the truth. I don't know who you saw or talked to tonight, but you can ask anyone in this town. My wife is dead. She died two years ago. I can show you her death certificate if that's what you need to believe me." I say as my voice threatens to break. She stares at me with wide eyes as I watch her try to process what I'm saying.

"She was here; a woman came here; she said she was your wife, tall with blonde hair." She says almost to herself. As she describes my late wife, I feel the nausea creeping up my chest.

"That's not possible, Dani." I don't even recognize my voice anymore because nothing makes sense. Angie is gone; there is no way she was here in this house. Unless she is haunting me, and I wouldn't be that surprised. The thought doesn't make the nausea any better.

"Do you have a picture of her? Something? I don't know. I'm not crazy, Jasper. I saw her; I fucking talked to her." She almost yells the words. I go into the desk and open the bottom drawer. The photo frame that used to sit on this desk sits at the bottom of it. I put it in here because I couldn't shake the feeling that her eyes were always watching me as I sat here. Walking over to Dani, I hand her the frame with the photo of my wife, and I watch as her already pale skin somehow gets paler.

"This is her, Jasper. She isn't dead. She was here tonight." She looks to me like I could explain this.

"Dani, I know for a fact she is dead. I'm the one who made the call that night. She was drinking; we had been arguing earlier that night. She was upset with me about my work. I went to bed angry, and I shouldn't have. But we had been fighting so much at that time in our relationship that I just gave up trying to fix things. She was jealous of everything, including the time I spent working. I could see the hate in her eyes for me, and no matter what I did, I just seemed to push her farther away. I hate to admit that I started to look at her the same way. She was a hateful woman towards the end, and I just couldn't let her go because I loved her. So, I just went to bed. I woke up to a loud sound and glass breaking." I try to explain the night, but I have to stop and catch my breath. I never thought I would have to explain this horrible night ever again. I sit behind the desk and put my head in my hands.

"When I came running out of the room, I didn't see her; it wasn't until I went to go downstairs that I saw her lying at the base of the stairs. Her neck was clearly broken, and I just knew, I fucking knew. I ran down the stairs, and when I checked, she was already gone. Even after all the hateful words she said to me and the things she did, it was the worst night of my life. So yeah, I'm sure she's dead." I say before looking up to meet her tear-filled eyes.

She comes around the desk and pulls my head into her stomach. "I'm so sorry, Jasper. I didn't know. How could I know? We don't ever talk about you. I don't even really know you." She says as I wrap my arms around her waist and look up at her.

"I know; we moved into all this so fast. I didn't want to mess anything up with my painful past." I say before she looks down at me and runs her hands through my hair.

"Your past is a part of you, Jasper. I want to know the good and the bad. I want to know you." She stares into my eyes, and I feel the tension release from my chest.

"Then know me, Dani. Give me a chance to show you who I am. Please don't leave. I know this is crazy, and the ghost of my ex-wife is a lot more baggage than you signed up for." I say with a small laugh. She tugs my hair back, forcing me to look at her.

"Hey, not funny. I'm not crazy. I still don't know what the fuck is going on, and I'm scared, Jasper. That woman was here. I told you before that I believe in ghosts, and she is not happy." She says, and I can tell she is questioning her sanity. I must admit I am right along with her because this can't be real. I lay my head back against her stomach and inhale her sweet scent.

"I know. She's always been a jealous woman. She's mad that I have you. A gorgeous, sexy, strong woman." I place kisses on her stomach with each word, and she leans her head back with a small laugh.

"This is not ok. She could be watching us. I don't know how I feel about being watched by ghosts. How am I supposed to work knowing some ghost doesn't want me here? She could be watching us right now." Her words have a slight trace of humor, but I can hear that she is genuinely concerned.

Looking up at her, I can see the fear in her eyes, and I smile. Slowly, I start to tug down the legs of her pants. Watching her eyes widen like she is about to protest what Im doing, I jerk them down fast and stand up quickly. Grabbing her behind the knees, I sit her on the desk.

"Let's give her a show then, her and any other ghost that walks the halls of this house. Because not even the dead can stop me from tasting you, Dani." I spread her knees apart and sit back in the chair. Rolling my chair to the desk where she sits spread open for me, I hook my hands behind her legs and dive my tongue deep into her sex. I suck and bite with a hunger that leaves her speechless. I try not to smile while I put on a show; I hope she is watching. Let her watch me worship this woman like she never let me worship her. As Dani comes undone on my office desk, the lights flicker, and I can't help but smile. Dani doesn't notice while in the euphoria of her release, but I do. Let her watch.

Chapter Fifteen

Dani

"I'm not ok, and I'm losing my mind," I say out loud as I misplace the tubing for the second time today. The past few days have been a blur as I try to work in a place where I am constantly feeling watched. Especially since Jasper likes to try and provoke the ghost wife by continually showing me affection. I don't shy away from his touch even though I initially wanted to. I saw that woman, she was here in this basement, and she was pissed.

"Come on, it's been days, and nothing has happened. Are you still spooked?" Jasper asks from the desk, and I look back at him like he's grown two heads.

"Jasper, at this point, I'm wondering if I need to make an appointment to check for a fucking brain tumor. I know what I saw that night. You can't blame me for being freaked out." I say as a chill courses through my body. The look in her eyes is burned into my brain, and I hate that I can't just push past it like him. I mean, this was his wife. The woman he said he loved, yet he provokes her by giving me mind-blowing orgasms daily in the house they shared. I'm into some pretty dark stuff, but I'm sure I'm crossing a line.

"What would make you feel better? You want me to call in the priests." He teases. The fact that he can make jokes isn't lost on me. I usually love his sense of humor, but something about it doesn't feel right. I know it's been years since she passed, and from what he says, their marriage was pretty much over at the time; it still just doesn't feel right.

"Ha, Ha, really funny. I'm sorry. I'm fine." I say, focusing back on my work. I can feel him come up to me as he wraps his arms around me.

"I'm sorry. I know it's weird; I just don't like seeing you so worried. If you needed time off, you could have taken it; you know that." He says, placing a soft kiss on my neck. I know he is just masking his emotions with humor, and I shouldn't hold that against him. I can't imagine how he must feel with me constantly bringing up the ghost of his wife. Fuck, this is so bizarre to even talk about her like her ghost actually exists, even though I know what I saw that night.

"No, I'm sorry. You're right; nothing has happened since then. Maybe I just inhaled too many fumes in here." I joke back, even though it still doesn't feel right. I know I'm lying to him and myself. His small laugh vibrates against my back as he places another kiss on my neck and pulls away. I continue to work when I hear the door behind me open. I turn around quickly to see him pause in the doorway.

"I was going to make those phone calls and finish filling that report. I can do it later if you don't feel comfortable down here alone." He says. I don't want him to think I can't even do my own job now. He will be right upstairs. I'm sure everything will be fine.

"No, it's ok, go ahead. If I get attacked by any spirits, I'll yell for you, so leave the basement door open." I tease even though I'm serious. He smiles, and I remember why I fell so quickly, the man is thoughtful and gorgeous. I don't know what happened the other night, but I need to try and move on from it. This is my job, and I can't let ghosts or delusions get in the way of why I'm here.

"I'll make us another pot of coffee while I'm up there." He calls out from the hallway as he leaves me alone in the embalming room. The body feels cold under my hands, but I feel the room get stuffy, the air thicker. I can tell myself to forget it all I want, but my body refuses. The room is quiet, and all I can hear is the faint buzz of the overhead light that seems to be cooking me all of a sudden. My hands stop, and I close my eyes, forcing myself to take a deep breath. "I am not crazy, I am in control of my emotions, and I need to get my shit together." My words echo in the silent room. When I open my eyes, I feel the tension release slightly, and I busy myself with my work. I can't stress like this every day. I'll tell Jasper we need to get a radio down here or something.

Tilting the body's head to start my incision, my hand freezes when I look past the body in the hallway leading to cold storage. The double door's small square windows are pitch black. I am frozen while I stare at those small dark windows, waiting for the doors to swing open. Have the lights been off this whole time? Could I have turned them off when getting Mr. Nelson's body? I wouldn't have done that; I never turn those lights off. Like a thousand tiny needles, my scalp pricks with the fear starting to course through my body. Starting to regain control of my body, I put the scalpel down and slowly back away, putting distance between me and the doors. My eyes never leave the small windows as I continue to slowly back away. The feeling of someone's eyes on me, staring out from the darkness, makes me feel like I just took an ice bath. I was beginning to sweat a moment ago, and now I can't stop the chills from running up and down my body.

My knees grow weak for a moment when the printer behind me starts to go off, and I finally take my eyes off the doors. The printer sounds so loud in this room, and I go behind the desk to see what is printing. We rarely use this computer or this printer in here. Looking back to the windows, I see the lights are back on, and I shake my head in disbelief. What the fuck is going on? The papers continue to print, and I pick them up from the printer, still looking to the now bright hallway beyond the double doors. Something is right here; I can feel it in my bones. Looking down at the papers, I flip through each one, and my heart sinks further with each piece of paper.

I

Tried

To

Warn

You

What the fuck is going on? When the room goes dark, I scream and drop the papers. Reaching my hands out to make my way into the darkness, I start to panic. Suddenly the lights kick on again, and I am running to the door leading out of this fucking room. Looking back, I run smack into Jasper in the hallway, not watching where I'm going.

"Hey, Hey, what's going on?" He hugs me tight, looking behind me. I can barely hear him, with my pulse thrumming in my ears.

"The printer. The fucking papers," I stammer while he looks at me like I'm crazy. Finally, I stop and try to control my breath. "The lights went out; the printer started printing these papers on its own, and it's her. I don't know if I can do this, Jasper. This is all too much." I'm still barely making sense, and now he looks concerned.

"What papers? Come show me." He tries to lead me back to the embalming room, but I freeze; I don't know if I can go back in there. This is some paranormal investigation shit, and I did not sign up for this. I know this is my job, but this is insane.

"I don't know if I can go back in there. I'm so sorry. I know this is my job, but we have to figure something out. I don't know what to do." I start to feel the tears sting my eyes, and the last thing I want to do is cry, but my body is in flight mode, and I just want to get out of this basement.

"Ok, it's fine. We will figure it out. I'm here with you now, and nothing will happen; just come and show me what's happening. I'm sure there is an explanation or something." He tries to console me, and I start to feel frustrated despite his trying to be nice. I want to get out of here. I don't want to explain anything or try to figure it out. I know what it is, and it's her, his wife. I know it's her, and I start to feel angry. It's not my fault she died; it was an accident. Why can't she let Jasper move on? I felt sorry at first, but now I'm just pissed that something so unbelievable as a ghost is coming between me and my job, my relationship. This is the kind of shit that happens in the movies, not in my life.

"Fine, I'll show you." Rolling my eyes, I push past him and lead the way back into the embalming room. He follows behind, and I can't help but feel like he doesn't believe me. Bending down, I pick up all the papers I dropped and start to flip through them for him. Page after page, I turn over, and the message that was there is gone. This can't be fucking happening.

"No, I know what I saw, Jasper; it said I tried to warn you. I saw it. The lights in the hallway to cold storage went out, and then the printer started going off printing that message. The lights even went off in here!" I flip through the pages again, even though I know the message is gone.

"Ok, how about we go have that coffee and take a break." He says, and my blood boils over.

"Don't you fucking look at me like that! I am not crazy. That psycho bitch is trying to make me look insane. I know what the fuck I saw!" I yell because I'm confused and angry.

"Dani, nothing is here on these papers. I don't know what to say. You have been under a lot of stress lately, and maybe.." He tries to finish, but I throw the papers at him.

"Fuck you. Don't treat me like I'm some burnt-out woman who can't control her emotions. I'm done." I start to walk away, knowing things will change when I leave this basement. I don't make it two steps before the door to the room slams shut. I jump back, staring at the door that just slammed shut on its own. Rushing to the door, I turn the knob, and it doesn't budge.

"Fuck!" I scream at the air, but it's cut short when the printer starts to go off again. I stare at Jasper, and his eyes are blown wide. "Can you explain that? Huh?" I say as I go to stand beside him, even though I want to strangle him right now. The papers continue to print, and he is looking at the door and the printer before he looks at me.

"I'm sorry, we will figure this out. Maybe it's something electrical I can stop this." He explains as he sits at the computer, trying to figure out why the printer is printing on its own. That won't explain the fucking door trapping us in the room. This room with no windows leading outside, no way of escaping unless that door opens. I feel the walls closing in when the papers start falling to the floor, the printer tray overflowing. Leaning down to pick up the papers, I see they are not empty this time. They are full of images, the documents still warm in my hands.

Looking at the images, I recognize the room, the stark blue light, and the table in the middle. I see the body on the table and a man standing beside it. The man moves in each image as my eyes bounce from frame to frame printed on these pages. My body shakes as I see this man place his hand on the body, on this body's breast, then down to the apex of her thighs. My breathing turns fast and shallow as I place my other hand over my mouth to stop myself from screaming. The man is on top of the woman, the angle of the image showing the glowing white skin of his ass as he appears to be thrusting inside of her. Her facial expression stays emotionless, while each image shows him throwing his head back in ecstasy. The room gets smaller, and I almost feel dizzy.

"Dani? What's wrong? Hey, are you ok?" Jasper stands up from the computer and approaches me, but everything seems like a blur.

"It's you. This is you." I flip through the pages as the images change, each one showing a new body but the same man. The same man that stands in front of me right now. The same man that has been inside of me. I feel the bile rise in my throat as he rips the papers from my hands. I back away, my body hitting the cold wall; I can't believe what is happening. This is all a trick; this is her way of tricking me, right? I watch in disbelief as Jasper flips through the images. Shaking his head in disbelief before looking up at me, a dark grin starts to tear across his face. My blood runs cold because he doesn't even look like himself anymore.

"You had to fucking do it, didn't you? You fucking bitch!" He throws the papers as his voice roars into the room. I close my eyes and try to melt into the wall. I need to get out of here.

"You just couldn't let it go, could you? You couldn't let me be happy!" Jasper continues yelling as he swings his arm, knocking over the tray of tools. This can't be happening.

Chapter Sixteen

Jasper

I'm blind with rage because I thought I had taken care of this. I thought I shut her up years ago, but here I am, trapped in a room with her accusations again. I feel like a caged animal, and I forget Dani is even in the room for a moment. There is no explaining myself, no way of getting out of this. Angie has returned and ruined everything; she was hellbent on destroying my life before she fell down the stairs and is even more determined in the afterlife. Is this karma? Is this what they mean when they say your past will come back to haunt you? Turning to Dani, I see her pressed against the wall, tears streaming down her face.

"Dani, please. This is...This is.." I try to find the words as her eyes pop open and look at me with a wave of fierce anger I've only seen once before.

"This is the fact that you are a fucking sick freak. That's what this is, Jasper. How could you? Is this what she is trying to warn me about? That you disrespect the bodies of dead women in this very fucking room!" She yells at me, and I want to go back to that first day. The first day we met, she looked at me with desire in her eyes. Her words sting and mimic the very same words Angie told me that night.

"I'm not a sick freak, Dani. Come on, look at me. I can explain. I made a mistake." I try to calm my voice as she stares at me.

"A mistake? Fucking dead bodies is not a mistake, Jasper! You're sick." She says, and although anger courses through every word, her lip trembles. I still want to pull her into my arms and kiss her pain away, even though I know I'm the one that caused it. I can't lose Dani; I can't let her leave until she understands why this happened. She is the reason I stopped doing this; she is the reason I regretted every body I touched that wasn't hers.

"Let me explain. Please. I was having a rough time in Angie and I's marriage. We weren't intimate long before the fights started. It had gotten to a point where we felt like fucking roommates; I couldn't have sex with my own wife. She wasn't affectionate at all, and the more I tried, the farther it felt like she pulled away." I explain, and she shakes her head at my words.

"That's no excuse. That explains nothing." She bites her words out.

"Please let me finish. One night a body came in, and it was someone I knew, someone from my past. Bethany Watz, I dated her in high school. She was my first love, the woman I probably should have ended up with if I wasn't such a dumbass when I was younger. She was funny and sweet, and it hurt to see her lying on that table." I start to explain.

"So you take advantage of her corpse? You aren't making this any better. I don't even know what to say to you." Dani says with eyes filled to the brim with tears.

"I was inspecting the body, and my hand grazed her breast; at first, I jerked back because it felt odd. I continued to work up the body, and at one point, it didn't feel like she was dead on the table. It was Bethany, she was still beautiful, and I swear I could hear her laugh in my ears. I touched her again and surprised myself at how my body started to react. It felt wrong for a moment, but Dani, I was so fucking lonely." I shake my head with my words remembering just how alone I felt. I felt alone in my marriage, and no one knows just how hard that is until they go through it. Dani doesn't say a word; she just puts her hand over her mouth.

"I knew Bethany, I loved her, and she loved me at one time. So, I gave in. I gave in to my body, crying out for a woman's touch, even if it was the cold touch of her body. It still felt warm to me because she was who she was. Someone I knew and loved. I made love to her, and when it was over, I felt ashamed. I knew what I did was wrong, even if it didn't feel that way. I remember I took over an hour in the shower scrubbing my skin raw because of what I had done—the temptation I had given into. I felt horrible but couldn't take back what I had done. The fact that I felt pushed to that point only made me resent Angie more. Our relationship only got colder, and it was months before I gave in again." I keep talking as I recheck the doorknob, thankful it's locked because I don't want Dani to leave.

"I don't want to hear anymore. I want to leave. Please, I can't." She starts to move towards the door, and I jiggle the handle for her again to show it's still locked. I continue to talk even if she doesn't want to hear it. She needs to. This is the only way we can move on.

"Please, once I'm done, you will understand. I swear I don't have some sick fetish for dead bodies. I prefer the warmth of your body, your expressions, and the sounds you make, Dani; I love you." I try to pull her into me, and she shoves me back.

"Don't, don't you dare." Her voice shakes as she backs against the counter.

"I can't describe what it feels like to be married to someone and feel so alone. I would talk to her and could tell she wasn't even listening. She didn't care about my work or my interests. She could care less. I think it was because we had tried to have a child for years, and it never happened. She wanted to adopt, and I didn't. After that, she quit having sex with me and quit trying. She hated me because I couldn't do the thing she wanted; I couldn't get her pregnant. I tried; I really did. I can't control something like that, you know? She hated me for it; I was a failure to her. Whenever I asked her if she wanted out of this, she would get upset and accuse me of not loving her. Then, she would flip it around. Everywhere I turned, I would lose, I would fail. Do you have any idea how that feels?" I ask and get no answer, just more tears, so I continue.

"So, one night, another woman comes in. I didn't know her, but she was beautiful." I cringe even saying the words because it all feels so wrong now. Nothing felt right until Dani; looking back now, I feel disgusting, but I can't change what I've done.

"My body betrayed my mind, and I was finding myself thinking about the time with Bethany, and I got aroused. I tried to push past it, but I longed for release. So I gave in again, and it was a little easier that time. The next time was even easier, and it had become a way to cope. Until one night, I was just starting, I was caressing the body, squeezing her chilled breast, when the door swung open, and Angie was standing there. She stared at me, and I didn't think she could look at me with more disgust. She stormed out, and I ran after her. She accused me of being a sick freak, and I didn't blame her. I begged for her forgiveness. I tried to explain to her that I felt so alone with her. We fought hard and told each other everything we had been holding back. I didn't tell her I actually had sex with the bodies, only that I was tempted that night, and that's the furthest I ever went. I thought she believed me. At the end of that fight, I felt a little lighter, and she agreed to be more affectionate. We had the best sex of our marriage that night." I laugh softly at the memory, the way she had me fooled. My mind travels deep into the memory, and I almost forget Dani is in the room.

"It didn't last, though. She had me fooled, thinking she was actually going to try and save our marriage. She pulled away again and threw what I did in my face every chance she could. I was right back to being a failure in her eyes, but now instead of just looking at me like she hated me, she looked at me with disgust. So, I fell right back into my old ways of coping. It wasn't all the time; as I said, I don't have some sick fetish for the dead. My mind didn't really choose, more like my body reacted, and I followed. What I didn't know was that she had planted something in here, and she recorded everything. She saw everything I did, everything I said. She put it all on this flash drive and made this big deal of sitting me down and playing it all back for me. Forcing me to watch myself do the things I was doing. I was mortified, embarrassed and guilty. She was angry and threatened to end my career, my life. She was going to out me to everyone. I had no choice." The tears start to fall at the memory of what I had to do. I didn't want to do it, but I knew I had no other way out.

"Oh, my god. No, don't tell me." Dani stares at me, and the lights flicker. I don't want to tell her anything else. I tried to avoid all this, but Angie would never let me. She won't let us out of this room until I come clean. That's what she wanted, to out me to the world. Her evil spirit won't rest until I come clean; I know in my heart that's what she wants.

"I have to. I don't think that door will open until I do. You understand, don't you? I made mistakes, but I had no choice. She was an evil woman Dani. But, please, it's still me. I'm still the man you trusted. You can still trust me." I beg her to understand.

"No, I don't trust you. I don't care how horrible your marriage was; nothing can excuse what you did to those bodies, and I don't want to hear anymore. Please, I want to get out of here." She moves to the door and pulls on the doorknob rattling the locked door.

"Let me out of here, please; this has nothing to do with me." She yells.

"Dani, please. Let me finish, and then you will understand, and we can get out of here." She looks back at me, and I know I have a lot of convincing to do to keep her.

"Angie was going to ruin my career.." I start to speak again, but she cuts me off.

"As she should have. You crossed the line, and not just once. You.." I don't let her finish; the anger boiling inside me spills over.

"Shut up and let me finish!" I yell, and I hate that she flinches at my words.

"Please, I just want this to be over so you can better understand everything, and we can get the fuck out of here, ok?" I ask, and she nods her head. So I continue even though my stomach is sick.

"Angie was going to turn in those files, proof of my moments of weakness. I couldn't let her do that. I tried to reason with her. I tried everything, and nothing was going to work. She had her mind made up on ruining me a long time before this, and now she had her proof. So, I did what I had to do to stop her from doing that." I say, hoping that's enough, trying to hide my deteriorating lack of patience. I mean, what else can I say? I know I did wrong, but the more I explain, the more upset Dani gets. She's looking at me the same way Angie did, and I'm trying to control the small burning anger growing inside me.

"Wait, what did you do? Did you fucking kill her? Tell me you didn't," Dani begs with tears in her eyes, and my heart breaks. I wish I could bring Angie back and kill her all over again for putting me through this. I never wanted to hurt Dani; everything was finally perfect.

"I did what I had to do. She was going to ruin my life, Dani. What was I supposed to do?" I ask, but I can see the horror on her face.

"Jasper, you killed your wife? You murdered someone? You're a monster. How could I not see this?" She asks the last question to herself.

"Because I made up my mind to change after that. At first, I could, but then my mind started its attack again. The guilt of what I had done to Angie and the urges battled in my head daily. So finally, I decided to hire an assistant who could take half the workload and give me more time away from the bodies. I never expected you to come into town and change everything. But you must know, Dani, when I met you, the thoughts stopped. The noise in my head disappeared, and you were like this cure. This beautiful, smart cure that changed me." I start to walk toward her, and she pulls back, shaking her head.

"That is why you hired me? To keep you from fucking dead bodies?" her lip trembles again with her words.

"No, well, yes, that is one reason, but I think fate had a bigger play in this. You needed to be saved from your trauma, and

I needed to be saved from my demons. We found each other, and you can't say things haven't been perfect. You would still want to be with me if my past didn't exist." I explain.

"But your past does exist. You did horrible things. It's hard enough to get passed the fact that you did that to those bodies. But you murdered someone. You can't look past murder. You can't ask me to do that." She tries the door again.

"Fuck why won't this open. He confessed! Right? Is that it? Please tell me that's it." She begs me.

"That's it. I haven't touched another person except you since you have been here. I haven't killed anyone else. I know these things are hard to look past, but I can't let you leave. I just can't. You are the only thing keeping the demons away. You are mine, Dani, you were meant for me, and I was meant for you. You know this is true." I tell her as she roams the room looking for something to pry the door open with. Suddenly she stops and looks at me.

"How did you do it?" She asks with a wince.

"I didn't lie about that; she fell down the stairs." If I tell her anymore there will be no coming back from this.

"You pushed her down the stairs. My god." She runs her hands through her hair, pacing.

"How did you get away with this? Tell me everything now. I want to know what you did." She is no longer crying; instead, she looks like she wants to kill me herself.

"I don't think that will help," I say.

"Do it, now! How did you kill your fucking wife, Jasper?" She yells

"I got her drunk, ok. I tied her up and poured cup after cup of liquor down her throat. Then after she was intoxicated enough, I pushed her down the stairs. The first time she fell, she was still alive. So I had to drag her body back up and push her again. That time was the last time it took. She broke her neck and died shortly after. It was believable because she was so intoxicated. Everyone knows everyone here, and they could never believe I would have done that. So, there. Are you happy now?" I yell, hating that I have to do this.

The door clicks, and Dani and I lock eyes; I don't wait for her to move; I rush to her. She makes it to the door before me and slams it into my body, knocking me back. Panic sets in that I can't let her leave. She moves quickly and makes it to the basement stairs before I grab her by the hair and pull her into my body.

"I don't want to hurt you. Please, stop. Don't make me do this. I care about you, about Alex. This can work if you just understand." I try to reason with her over her struggling in my arms.

I only have eyes for you.

The music blares so loud I'm sure anyone passing outside could hear it. I have to turn it off. I push past Dani, shoving her down the last two steps before I reach the top of the stairs and shut the basement door. I will keep her down there until she can calm down. I won't let her leave until she understands I'm not the bad guy. I changed, I worked really fucking hard, and I changed. My thoughts run rampant as I storm through the house, trying to find the source of the music. The music's volume and my heartbeat make my ears ring, and I'm delirious on rage.

"Shut up. Shut up, you fucking bitch. You ruined everything! I changed. I fucking changed. But damn it, I would kill you again if I could for this Angie." I yell, wishing she would show herself so I can wrap my hands around her throat.

"Angie fucking stop this," I yell.

My world is crashing down around me, and the weight of it is almost too much to bear. I was so close.

Chapter Seventeen

Dani

I've never felt so many emotions battling to take over in my body before. I'm scared, scared of the man I thought I could trust. Terrified that he is going to kill me because now I know he is capable of murder.

I'm angry that I ever believed I could live a normal life. Furious that I am stuck in a basement while the man I thought I was falling in love with screams at the ghost of his wife upstairs.

I'm disgusted by the things he did and the fact that I let those same hands touch my body. Disgusted that a man like him, who seemed so perfect, could be capable of doing the vile things he did. How could those hands that touched me so tenderly be capable of these things?

Something shatters from above, and I back away from the stairs; I am trapped in here. How could I not see what was right in front of my face? I never asked him if he was married or had kids. I didn't ask any questions that would have started a conversation about his past. I was blinded by lust and the promise of something normal. Would he have told me the truth? I doubt it. If I did the things he did, I could never admit it; I could never speak the words to explain what I have done. I wish I could feel sorry for him and his sad story about his loveless marriage, but I can not muster up any shred of pity. I have none.

Fear is the only thing I have right now coursing through every vein in my body, seeping out of every pore. This basement used to be where I felt powerful, thriving in my career. That power is gone, and the area feels more like a prison now. I search the room for anything I can use as a weapon. Leaving the office area, I return to the embalming room, remembering the scalpel I had. Could I actually use it on Jasper? The image of Alex alone at home, wondering where I am, flashes in my mind. The light bounces off the shiny tool in my hand, and I know that I would sink it deep into his neck if it meant getting back to my brother.

Everything leading up to this moment feels so dirty now. I really thought he would be someone I could have a real relationship with. A man that looked like he was created just for me, handsome and polite but still dark and mysterious. I had no idea just how dark he was or the secrets he was hiding in these walls. I can't blame myself too much because he has this whole town fooled. I think back on Mrs. Janet's words, how she felt sorry for him and was happy we found each other. She thought he deserved love, not knowing the things he had done. He has everyone fooled, and it's because he doesn't look like the type that would do something like this. He isn't your stereotypical murderer or necrophiliac; he is a modern Ted Bundy, handsome and well-kept, while completely fucked in the head. I know he isn't a serial killer, but he killed. Once is enough to convince me that he is a monster and that I must find a way to get out of here.

The music stops, and I back away, subconsciously wanting to put as much space between us as possible. The basement door slams shut, and my body jolts with panic as I hide the scalpel behind my back.

"Dani?" he calls my name from the hallway, and each footstep I hear makes me dizzy with fear. I don't have control of my body anymore as I move backwards down the hallway to cold storage. The cold air hits my back and envelopes around me. I look around at this room with no windows and no way of escaping; I am a caged rat. The bodies lie to my left, witnesses to my downfall.

The doors creak open as Jasper walks in; he looks different now. The eyes I thought were dark and sexy now feel menacing and haunted.

"I'm sorry for all of this. I never meant for any of this to happen. You know that, right?" He says as we circle each other.

"I won't say anything. I just want to leave." I say the words I've heard a dozen times in movies. They never let you leave.

"I don't know if I can do that, Dani. I don't know if I can trust you."
He explains.

"But you want me to trust you?" I ask. He smiles, and the bile I
have been forcing back down rises again, burning my throat.

"I want you to understand that I'm still me. I am still the man you
met that first day. I made some mistakes in my past; who hasn't?
I'm not some killer, Dani. I only did what I did to protect what we
have now. If I hadn't, you wouldn't be here, working here. None of
this would even exist anymore. Angie was going to take it all away.
I protected what was mine, what is ours now." He steps closer,
and my skin burns with heat. My hand wraps tightly around the
scalpel hidden behind my back.

"Please, I won't say anything. Just let me leave. Think of Alex and
what he's been through. You said you cared." My chest feels like it
sinks at the mention of Alex's name; he needs me. Jasper moves
closer, and my hand grips tighter on the tool.

"I know, which is why this hurts so damn much. I was better; I
wasn't touching anyone but you. I promise. I was making the steps
to stop what I was doing. I made a mistake. I was a lonely old fool,
and I fucked up." He tries to sound soft, but his words still cut
deep.

"It's not just that, Jasper; it's the fact that you murdered someone, your wife. How could I ever feel like we are safe with you?" The lights flicker at the mention of her, and the tension in the air is palpable. I watch as Jasper's face turns dark and angry.

"My wife was a miserable bitch who, even in the afterlife, wants me to be miserable as well. She is just jealous of what we have." His voice echoes loudly, talking to me but mostly to her. I need to get out of this room; the lights flicker again. Panic burns my chest, and I start to feel the walls closing in. I'm getting out of here.

"What we had! There is nothing here anymore. I want to fucking leave now." I scream at him as I try to figure out a way around him.

"I can't do that, Dani. I love you. I know that sounds crazy. I know how all this looks, but I promise I can fix it. Don't let the past keep us from something so perfect. Think of the life I could give you and Alex." I want to cut his tongue right out of his mouth.

"I don't need you to give Alex and me a life; I made one for myself. I take care of him. Not you." I let my anger drip from every word as he shakes his head at me. The room gets colder, and I fight the urge to wrap my arms around myself.

"I admire that about you. You take care of what's yours and would do anything to protect it, right? We are similar in that way. Come on, let's stop all this. Let's go back to the way things were. I can fix this. Let me fix it." He softens his words and closes the distance between us. Trying to pull me into his arms, I push away, scared to use the weapon behind my back. He backs me into the cold storage containers, and my arms feel trapped behind me as he presses his body into mine, tucking my hair behind my ear.

"I love you; let me take care of all this. I will fix this." He repeats for the thousandth time and a sickening panic sets in when he moves to kiss me. I lose control of my body, and it just reacts, swinging the sharp edge of the scalpel as it slices effortlessly through the skin of the arm caging me in. I hear him hiss in pain as I push off the containers and try to reach the door. I feel my neck crack as he pulls my hair, almost knocking me off my feet. The scalpel falls as he pulls me back against the containers. I feel both of his hands run up the side of my head, digging into my hair before he slams my head into the wall.

"You stupid bitch, how could you?" He yells, but his voice sounds like it's miles away.

"I was going to give you everything!" I see his face contorted with anger before I feel another blow to the back of my head. He steps away, running his hands through his hair as I feel my body slide down the wall. I feel like I'm underwater and can't find the strength to swim up to the surface. The fuzzy image of him pacing the room is all I can see, the corners of my vision blurry and distorted. This is the end. This is where I will die. I will never leave this place; I will never see my brother again. I tried so hard to change our lives, not knowing that I was always destined to fail. Every hand of cards I was dealt was already fixed so that I would lose.

My ears ring, and my vision fades in and out. Then everything goes black. Am I dead? I still hear the muffled sounds of Jasper's voice.

"What the fuck is going on. HEY!" I hear him but can't see anything; my world has gone black. Suddenly a warm orange light shines from across the room, the air gets hotter, and I blink rapidly, trying to clear my vision.

"Let me go; what the fuck is this?" I can still hear him yelling from some far-off place.

Then a voice comes through the fog, clear and crisp. "Get up, my little raven; you have to get up. Get out of here. Pull yourself up. You can do this. Let's go." The words spring tears to my eyes. I know that voice, the voice I haven't heard in years. The voice I would have paid anything to hear just one more time.

"Daddy?" I question my sanity, but somehow I am moving my body.

"Get out of here, Now! Move, Dani," his voice booms in my head, and I'm moving slowly, but I'm finally standing upright. When I look through the darkness, I blink several more times to try to make sense of what I see. The crematory light is on, and the flames are glowing in the room. Jasper screams as he backs himself up step by step toward the fire.

"Stop; I'm sorry. Please. Don't do this." His voice is filled with panic, and I'm frozen, watching him being pulled by some unseen force toward the heat of the crematory. Then as if two hands wrap around his midsection, he folds, still screaming. Tears feel hot against my cheeks as I hear the loud snap of his bones over his screaming. The door to the flames stays open, lighting the room as his body burns in the fire. I'm stuck watching until the smell of burning flesh invades my senses and pushes me to move.

Smoke flows out of the doors behind me as I clumsily run down the hall through the basement. Reaching the top of the stairs, I remember the chemicals in the basement and the flames licking out of the small door. The realization has me pushing my body out the door and stumbling down the steps, putting distance between me and that house. My lungs feel tight, and my head feels heavy, but I reach the sidewalk.

"Help, please." I may pass out, and right as the neighbor comes outside to see what the commotion is about, a loud boom vibrates the ground under my feet. Falling to the sidewalk out of pure exhaustion, I feel hands on me. I panic until I see it's just the neighbor before I allow the world to fade to black all over again.

Chapter Eighteen

Dani

Application Accepted

I stare at the glaring words across the screen; this is the third application I put in this morning. Unfortunately, Cooley's Mortuary was the only one within miles, which explains why we were always so busy. I don't mind traveling for work if it means I don't have to uproot Alex and me all over again.

The town took the loss of its upstanding citizen, Jasper Cooley, pretty hard. I pass by the little memorial people put up and try to stomach the nausea that rolls through me like a tidal wave. Yet, I have moments when I actually miss him. Crazy huh? I miss the man that tried to kill me in his basement. Maybe I am more like my mother than I'd like to admit. But I guess it's because I have to pretend to miss him in front of everyone.

I didn't tell anyone Jasper's dirty little secrets. I don't know why I made that choice; I just felt like the way he went out was punishment enough. I still question if I'm insane or if I really did watch him get pulled into the flames. The memory of the smell hits me all over again, and I am reminded that it really did happen.

"Morning," Alex calls as he enters the kitchen. He has been so supportive and understanding in all of this. Although I can see the worry in his eyes sometimes, I'm sure it's because he knew how I felt about Jasper and knows I'm out of a job now. He comes to sit with me in the living room, and the smell of his near-burnt pop-tart fills the room.

"Any responses?" he motions to my laptop, the words still staring at me.

"None yet, but I'm sure I'll hear something by next week. Don't worry." I close the screen and push it aside. I know he's worried about what happens next. I'd be lying if I said I wasn't concerned also. It's been almost two weeks since the fire took over and burned down Cooley's Mortuary, along with all its secrets. I told everyone I was upstairs in the office when I smelled the smoke, and when I tried to get to Jasper, the flames had already taken over downstairs. No one suspected me of anything other than being heartbroken.

Part of that was true; I am heartbroken, but maybe not for the reason they believe. My heart breaks for the life I thought I would have out here that's slipping through my fingers. Looking at Alex scarf down his breakfast, I remind myself that I made it out of that house, and that's what matters. I made it out of the house that was filled with a mother who let me down time and time again. I made it out of the house that held secrets that weren't my own, that wanted to take me down with it. I made it; I survived. It's hard to remind myself to be grateful when it still hurts so much.

"I'm not worried. I know you will find something. I'm more worried about you. You haven't talked much about everything. You know you can talk to me, right?" he says.

Images of Jasper's screaming face flood the room, and I shake them off. I can never tell Alex what truly happened. I can never tell anyone because no one would believe me. I barely believe myself sometimes.

"I know, I'm fine. It's a sad thing that happened, but I'll be alright. We will be alright." I assure him when the knock at the door comes.

"I'll get it." He says, tapping my leg. I'm sure it's Mrs. Janet again, she has been bringing over food the past week, worried about us. I swear, if angels exist, she is one of them. I stand up when I hear a man's voice, but Alex is already letting the man in. I don't recognize him as he stands in my foyer, dressed in a suit.

"Miss Brooks?" he says my last name, and now I'm nervous. Is he a detective? Does he think I had something to do with the fire?

"Yes," I try not to sound defensive, but I can't help it. Alex stands next to me, and the man stares at us both for a moment before speaking again.

"I'm sorry, you're just so young. My name is Carter Morris. I'm Mr. Cooley's executor." He explains.

"His what?" Alex's eyes go wide.

"I'm sorry, his legal representative of sorts. Can I have a minute with you, Miss Brooks?" he gestures to the living room, and I agree. Am I in trouble? I want to tell Alex to go upstairs, but part of me wants to keep him close. I don't know what this is about, and my chest fills with anxiety. We all sit down, and I watch him pull papers from some folder. I'm still confused when he starts to speak.

"I'm here to talk about Mr. Cooley's documentation; his letter was found seemingly untouched by the fire. I was made aware of it and made the necessary revisions." He hands me the piece of paper, scorched on the edges by the fire. I can smell the smoke on the page, and my stomach turns. Blinking back tears, I read the letter in my hands. My brain only picks up pieces as the room seems to tilt.

Leave everything to my little raven, Danielle Brooks.

Estate

Cooley's Mortuary

"What is it?" Alex's voice pulls me back, and I'm speechless. I recognize those words, the exact words that pulled me out of that house.

My little raven.

How is this possible? My father's words on a paper signed by Jasper sits in my hands. I blink back more tears holding the letter to my chest, not wanting Alex to see the nickname he would recognize on the paper.

"It appears that Mr. Cooley was very fond of you. If you don't mind me saying, I have been his advisor for many years, and I am happy he was able to find love again. He was a mess after Angie. It's a pleasure to meet you. I just need you to sign a few things, and I'll be on my way." The man's voice, although gentle and sweet, sickens me. He has no idea the man he represented was the cause of Angie's death. Was it really pain or sadness Jasper felt after Angie's passing? Or was it guilt disguised as pain? None of us will ever know.

"I'm sorry, I'm just still a little shocked. I had no idea about any of this. What exactly does this mean?" I ask.

"Mr. Cooley, in his passing, has left his estate, business, and remaining funds in the sum of...." He explains, but his voice becomes a distant thing, and I watch as Alex's face falls. I know he wants to be there for me, but I can't help but see the relief in his eyes, making the tears fall much easier.

I sign the papers, and Mr. Morris promises to contact me with the rest of the documents. Turning away from the door, Alex pulls me into a hug, and we both cry. We won't say it, but these tears are not for Jasper; these are tears of relief. This changes everything. My father's voice was there with me that night; his love is still with us today. I don't know how death works; I don't know much of anything anymore. All I know is even after you stop breathing and your body turns cold, the one thing that lives on is love.

Epilogue

The air always feels lighter in a bookstore. I haven't been here in over a year now. The bookstore in town was linked heavily to his memory in my mind. Somehow I thought I would walk through the store and see his spirit between the shelves. I always feel like he is watching me; it doesn't feel malicious, just sad now.

When they started rebuilding on the lot, I was nervous, and I still am. I feel like once the new mortuary is open, he will haunt me the same way Angie haunted him. But I don't think he will carry the same hate for me as Angie did for him. If his spirit is somehow still around this town, he will know that in the year since his passing, I still haven't told a soul about the secrets he held close. I haven't tarnished his clean reputation at all. Why should I?

We live the lives we were given, and we try like hell to do it right. But, no matter how amazing it appears to someone else, it's never easy. Everyone has secrets and problems; we are all fighting to survive in one way or another. Life doesn't care about your feelings or how much money you have in your bank account. I know Jasper had problems that, while I don't understand and probably never will, it is not my place to judge. How he coped with life was disgusting, desperate, and sad, but we all are looking for ways to cope. Some of us form addictions to numb the pain. Some of us throw ourselves into work, hobbies, and even books as distractions from the pain. In Jasper's case, he sought out affection to mend his pain, even if it was from a cold, lifeless body. I try to understand why he did the things he did, and I always come up empty.

I scan the shelves of the aisle of non-fiction books; usually, I'd be on the other side of the store where the horror novels are stacked, but today, I am searching for a gift. My finger scans the spines, searching for the title I'm looking for, Spiritual Junkie, a book for my mother. She has been in rehab for the past four months, and she reached out to us during her second month there. I almost hung up the phone; I still don't know why I didn't. The anger is still there, but I can't help but be proud of her; fighting for her sobriety isn't easy, and she has become very spiritual since then, So it's hard to argue with someone when they are so fucking zen. I find the book I'm looking for and make my way to the counter; I make a mental note to come back and browse the shelves when I have more time. We are going to do our first visit today in person with mom; Alex is nervous, and so am I. So, I thought a gift might break the ice a little.

The door to the backroom opens, and I'm greeted by a man who looks like a much younger version of Mr. Mitchell. He's taller but wears the same small frame glasses as Mr. Mirchell. The chestnut brown curls sit on top of his head, with a jawline that could chisel stone; I wonder if this is what Mr. Mitchell looked like when he was younger.

"Did you find what you were looking for?" He asks as he starts to ring me up.

"Yeah, I'm sorry, but is Mr. Mitchell still here?" I don't know why I asked that. This must be his son, and what if he died or something? I'm ready to apologize when he starts to speak again.

"The old man finally retired. I'm Micheal, his son. I guess you could say I took over the family business." He smiles and offers me his hand.

"Nice to meet you; I'm Dani," I take his hand, introducing myself.

"You live in town?" he asks.

"Yeah, I moved here a little over a year ago." Answering as I pay for the book.

"I just moved back. I thought I would like it out there, but it turns out there is nowhere else quite like Ripville Falls." He says with a small laugh.

"I have to agree with you on that one," I say. He bags my book but doesn't hand me the bag immediately.

"Do you know anyone looking for a job? I plan to put an ad out, but word of mouth travels faster in this town. I don't know how my dad ran this place alone for so many years." He asks.

"I have a brother who just turned sixteen and is looking for a part-time job. I tried to get him to work for me, but he isn't a fan of my line of work. I own the mortuary." It still feels weird saying that I own anything. Micheal's face contorts, and he hands me the bag.

"Oh god, I don't blame him. I couldn't be around dead bodies all day. If I can help it, I'd rather never be around one. Send him my way; I can use the help." He says with a laugh, and the fact that dead bodies freak him out makes me laugh too.

"Thank you, I'll let him know. It was nice to meet you, Micheal." I start to leave, and he calls out as I reach the door.

"I'll let dad know he had a pretty girl stop by asking for him. He should get a kick out of that." He says with a flirtatious smile. I smile back with a wave of goodbye and head home to get Alex. My cheeks feel flush at the compliment from Micheal, but the cool, crisp air cools my warms them as I walk home. I use the walk home to look around and appreciate where we are. Sometimes, it still doesn't feel real. The road here was long, but we made it, and

I could finally breathe. Life is giving me a break, and I hope it's a long one this time. I think back to the handsome face behind the counter of the bookstore. I'm not sure I'm ready to date again, ever. But if I do, at least I know how he feels about dead bodies. I laugh to myself because my life could be a movie or one hell of a book.

The End

The End

Made in United States
Troutdale, OR
04/14/2024

19181463R00100